In Love With A Rap Star

In Love With A Rap Star VOL: 1

Twala Meju

Thaimani Group

Published by The Thaimani Group
P.O. Box 1706
Conyers, GA 30012
Info@thaimanigroup.com

Printed in the United States of America
Designed by Denominator Graphics
Cover Photo by Francis Gasparro Photography

PUBLISHER'S NOTE
This book is a work of fiction. Names, characters, places, and incidents either are the product of the author's imagination or are used fictitiously, and any resemblance to actual persons, living or dead, business establishments, events, or locales is entirely coincidental.

Acknowledgments

First and always first-God for giving me the gift of words. I've been in love with you from the moment I heard your name - Jesus. My husband and children: Thairiq and Amani, for enduring microwave dinners and postponed trips during my times of writing. I did it all for us (Smile!) Now mommy can finally take you somewhere without a pen and notebook.

My mother, the women who gave me life and whom I would return the same gift. You are my strength when I'm weak and you are my light when the days are dark. My daddy for your infinite wisdom and giving me that pedestal to stand on. My brother Jamar thanks for everything. I owe you everything. If you ever need a kidney I GOT YOU. My brother Earl for your technical and engineering skills-you really are from another planet- I LOVE YOU. My brother Rollo(Rollohustle), you are everything I could have hoped for. You made everything come together and thanks for keeping me up on Miami's lingo.

My grandmother for giving me inspiration when I thought I would crack up before I'd had a chance to finish this book. All of my aunts, uncles and cousins; too many to name, your unconditional love is my existence. Melvin "Mel Man" Breeden- we've come a long way from being sent to Neveda with no money (We can laugh at those days now!!) Leroy McMath for giving an inexperienced girl a chance to be apart of this wonderful life we know as the music industry. Dionne, for being there from the beginning. Just don't forget me when you get famous.

My manager, Carol Brown of The Lorac Media Group - a storm to be reckoned with. Tre Davenport of Tre

Day PR- What an amazing spirit!! Thanks for being a part of my writing career. Cherry Banez-You work too hard...let's take a vacation. Pam Pinnock of Lip Service Media. Elora Mason of E. Mason & Associates-The Queen of Miami.

Allen Johnston-The Music Specialist; I could be here all day but I was told to keep it short. What you have done for me and taught me would take me three lifetimes to repay. I've learned so much from you and your knowledge never ceases to amaze me. Big T-I'll never forget how you allowed us to ball out of control in Palm Springs, CA.- www.freebaruti.org. Q-for always worrying about me. Cherelle-the realest diva I know (Saturday Love). Kyle Norman of Jagged Edge and Sean Paul of The Young Bloodz- you're still the same guys I remember growing up with. I 'm proud of who you've become and will forever be your biggest supporter.

C-Murder-I can't thank you enough. Not only are you a phenomenal artist but your life story inspires me. Si Asia-thanks for the fly wardrobe. Janice Mcfadden (Cucumbers have thorns and Snakes love Strawberries), Leroy Decosta, Janice Sims, G-dinero, Bigga Rankin, Francis Gasparro, Kesley and Torry of 2 Brothers Real Estate, Sylvia, Dan the Man of Denominator Graphics. Not only are you the best artist I know but you are a true friend that has always kept it real, whether I wanted to hear it or not. If I forgot anyone please charge it to my mind not my heart. A special thanks to all of you who purchased "In Love With A Rap Star VOL I." I hope you enjoy it as much as I enjoyed writing it!!!!

To the rapper who gave me my start in
the music industry ☺

Chapter One

"Ring Ring Ring," the phone sounded. I looked at the clock, who could be calling at three in the morning? "Hello," I answered still half asleep. "Girl, you won't believe who I saw Sean at the club with tonight." I jumped up as though these words were an instant alarm. "Club! What are you talking about you saw Sean at the club tonight? He's at the Hit Factory this week." "What he was doing didn't have nothing to do with no Hit Factory," Monica said, making it sound worse than it probably was. "Who was she," I demanded to know. "Just get up and get dressed; I'm on the way to get you."

"Okay, but let me at least call him first." "Angel, you never give a man time to get rid of the evidence. You're gonna get in my car and we are gonna roll up on his lying and trifflin ass." "Monica I don't know about this." "Angel you have to stop letting this man walk all over you, besides I'm outside." I pulled my hair back into a ponytail and slipped on my *House of Dereon Jeans* and *Sneakers*. "What am I doing," I asked myself.

"Beep Beep," Monica's car horned echoed through the neighborhood. "Hurry up let's go," she yelled.

Taking a deep breath, I slowly opened the door not knowing if I was ready to face what I had known for years. I closed the door without looking back and hopped in the back seat of Monica's Jeep Cherokee. "Why are you sitting in the back? Do I look like a chauffeur," Monica asked. "Yes, especially when you're pulling me out of my bed at three in the morning. What are you even doing out this late anyway?" "You better be glad I was out

1

this late or you would still be in the dark." "Monica why can't you just tell me who she is and let me handle it my way." "Because I know your way and it will never get handled."

It took us five minutes to get there, but it seemed like our summer vacations driving from Florida to New York on the last day of school. Monica pulled up to a house with cars lined up and down the street.

"What's going on here? Whose house is this anyway?" "Just get out the car and come on." "I can't my legs won't move. What if he's really here with her?" At that moment Monica begin to have second thoughts about hurting her friend, but only for a moment because she pulled me out of the car and bum rushed the front door. The first person Monica saw was Todd, as she pushed open the door.

"Don't come up in here acting all Ghetto Fabulous," Todd warned. "Man shut up, where's your boy?" "Who?" "Don't play dumb because you see his girl standing here; you know exactly who I'm talking about." It was like pulling teeth, but to avoid an explosion with Monica, Todd reluctantly gave up the information. "Monica my heart is beating so fast; I can't do this." "Angel pull yourself together," said Monica trying to calm my nerves.

The sounds got louder and louder as Monica and I walked upstairs. I recognized Sean's raspy, New York accented voice. "Yeah right there." Rivers of tears started to fall from my eyes as a soft voice whispered, "It's yours Sean." Monica squeezed my hand and started wiping the tears from my face. "Don't give this bastard the satisfaction of seeing you cry."
I could no longer stand there and listen to what Sean had told me two days ago. I burst through the door and flipped the lights on, as

eight years of wrong numbers, hang ups, so called studio sessions and "she's just a fan" excuses started rolling through my head.

Sean jumps up as if he were waking up from a bad dream. Thoughts of killing them both ran through my mind. I could take them out, go home to grab my passport and be in Jamaica by tomorrow.

"Sean, what the hell is going on here? Tasha? This has got to be some kind of sick joke. I'm being punked right," I said waiting for Ashton and the cameramen to walk in.

"Angel I'm sorry. I...I didn't want you to find out this way," Tasha said hiding behind Sean. I would expect this from any other bitch on the street but you; you're my cousin Tasha. How could you do this to me? We're like sisters."

"What's that suppose to mean?" "It's suppose to mean sisters don't open their legs for each others men. And to think, I gave you a place to live when Dre kicked you out and your mother wanted nothing to do with you. I was the one who cried with you and I stayed on my knees praying to God about your troubles more than you did. And this is how you repay me for all of that? And Sean?"

"Baby let me explain," Sean said nervously. "Oh, I'm your baby now, when were you going to tell me you were messing around with my cousin?" "Messing around, oh she doesn't know," Tasha interrupted. "Know what," Monica and I said in unison. "From where I'm standing and what I think is about to go down up in here I would say as least as possible," Monica snapped.

Ordinarily Tasha would have taken Monica's advice but with Sean standing in between them her balls grew bigger. "Well, since everything is out in the open, remember when I told ya'll I didn't know who my babies daddy was, well, they all belong to Sean. He thought it was best to announce it at our engagement party next month," Tasha gloated.

"Hold up! Sean's whose father," I asked in a state of confusion. "The girls." "Did you know this before or after you asked me to be with you in the delivery room?" "Before." "What were your motives for having me there? So everybody would know what a fool I was for being there for a woman that was having my man's kids. Who else knew about this?"

"Just Sean and I," Tasha replied. "For God's sake I'm their godmother." "I want to know about the engagement," Monica asked, wanting to get everything out on the table. "Bitch where's your ring," I asked, showing her my five carat diamond. "You don't even know where this man lives," I snapped. "I have his babies and that's enough," Tasha said snapping back.

I wasn't the type to fight over a man because my theory was why fight for something that is already yours, but if you crossed that line of disrespect you were begging for an ass wippin. Before Monica and Sean knew what happened, I had flipped Tasha over the bed and gave her the life lessons that her mother should have taught her on what could happen if you mess with another woman's man. It took both of them to pull me off of her. I had to instantly catch my breath because I was far from finished with Sean.

"So you're around here popping out babies, but when I told you I was pregnant you told me it wasn't the right time because it would ruin your career. It was because of your dumb ass I got pregnant in the first place, throwing away my birth control pills as soon as I got them and refusing to use condoms. What the hell did you think would happen? You know how bad I wanted to keep that baby. Do you even realize what that has done to me? It's not a day that goes by that I don't think about that baby," I reflected. It took me four years to tell him this. After I came home from the clinic he behaved as if it were a forbidden secret. Angel Eyes is what he called me when he knew he was caught up in a lie and trying to get back in good with me. "Angel Eyes, I know how you feel, I think about it too. I think about how our lives would have been so different, married with a child and a phat crib in Atlanta."

"Well, while everyone's dreaming of what could or should have been. This is reality for your ass. Sean and I have four beautiful girls and we will be married," Tasha interrupted. "Bitch please, this has nothing to do with you right now," Monica snapped. "Sean is this true?" He looked away contemplating his confession. "Don't you think you owe me that much?"

Sean asked Tasha and Monica to leave the room so he could state his case without objections. "Hell no, I'm not leaving you with this nut; Angel lets just go," advised Monica.

"No Monica it's cool; I need to hear this." "Okay if you need me I will be right by the door. Do you hear that Sean? Right by the door!"

Monica reluctantly left with Tasha not too far behind. As soon as the door slammed, Monica began reading Tasha her rights.

"You's a dirty bitch. That's your cousin, how could you do that to her after everything we went through with her after her parents died. We were like sisters and you gonna trade all of that for some dick. Niggas come and go, but blood is thicker than water."

"I knew you would never understand. I've never had someone that didn't judge me about my past and accepted the baggage that came along with me," as Tasha begin to cry.

"You had Dre." "Dre doesn't count." "Tasha, you're dumber than you look. That man in there loves everybody, do you honestly think you and Angel are the only females he's messing around with," said Monica so bluntly. "Yes, he has no reason to lie to his wife."

"Trick please, you're calling yourself his wife now. I guarantee you will never make it down the isle. I bet he is in there already thinking of ways to get Angel back on the team. He's far from dumb, the only reason he would consider marrying you is because he knows those child support payments would be coming for his ass," Monica admitted. "Whatever," Tasha said with disappointment.

"Angel Eyes I never meant to hurt anyone especially not you." Hearing the truth versus suspecting the truth was harder to digest than I thought it would be. "Yes their mine. I wanted to keep her from telling you and you finding out from the tabloids, so I told her I would do the right thing and make her my wife. I only told her what she wanted to hear. It's not like it was really going to happen.

Angel I love you more than my last breath, but I messed up and I didn't know how to tell you," Sean confessed.
"Sean how did this happen? When? Where? Why?" Sean moved in closer to grab my hands but I pulled away as if an incurable disease infected him. "Baby I don't know where to start." "You can start at how you ended up with four kids while you and I were together." "Angel, this isn't easy to say, please sit down."

"On the bed you just got finished screwing my cousin on. You're smoking right?" "Nah Nah. Maybe that was a bad suggestion," he said walking towards the bathroom to flush the condom down the toilet.

"It started almost three years ago, the night you left for California. I figured you were still upset about our argument so I came by with champagne and roses to apologize. Tasha met me at the door and told me you were in LA. I was irate because you didn't even tell a nigga you were flying out. She started talking about how wrong Andre was doing her and I started talking about our problems. We started drinking she kissed me and one thing lead to another." "You son of a bitch," I said trying to slap the shit out of him. "I deserved that." "I'm tired of people using alcohol to justify sleeping around. You slept with her because that's what you wanted."

"Baby just listen to me," he said pulling me up to him. "I'm listening, speak your peace but I really need you to back up off of me right now." "I don't know how it went this far. You know I'm in love with only you; just tell me how I can make this right. I'll do anything to have you back." "Are you kidding me? I was the perfect wife without the vows. What was it? Did I love you too much, not enough? I don't understand." "All my boys know you are my trophy wife, I just got caught up."

"What do you mean you'll do anything to get me back? Do you not keep mental records of your lies? Didn't you just say you had to do the right thing and make Tasha your wife?" "Yeah, but just say the word and that's done," Sean swore. "So you're telling me that all I have to do is say the word and you would leave Tasha and your four children for me," I said in disbelief.

"Angel Eyes, you don't have to say much, just say you forgive me and we can leave tonight. I wanna give you my last name and my first son. I'll buy us that dream house in Atlanta for the winter and the little villa we stayed in off the South of France for the summer. Just give me this last chance and I promise…" I put my finger on his lips before he could mesmerize me anymore with his promises. "Sean that's all I ever wanted to hear, but it should not have taken this for you to realize I'm the only one you want." "Alright, cool so I'll have Lopez get the jet ready for us to leave tonight," as he rudely interrupted.

"Sean slow down; you're getting ahead of yourself. I can't possibly be with you after this. I could never trust you again and besides I could never be with a man that puts a woman before his children."

Tears begin to roll down his face. I knew he was sincere. There were only two times in eight years that I had seen him cry; at my parent's funeral and the day I had to abort our child. "Sean I have to go. I can't do this right now. I have a lot to think about." "Don't go!" "I have to get out of here and clear my head."

"I can't let you go you're all I have in my life that's real." "You don't have a choice," I said snatching my arm from his hand; not knowing what he had done with them.

By this time he was begging harder than a female groupie trying to get pass backstage security at a Snoop Dogg Concert. "Really, is this necessary?" "Just tell me you'll think about it," he said with desperation in his voice.

"Yeah, sure Sean; now can I please leave." As I pulled the door open, Monica and Tasha fell in from eavesdropping. "You two deserve each other," I said looking Tasha in her face. She quickly got up with the sheet still wrapped around her naked body and ran to Sean's side attending to the red bruise I left on his face. "I'm good," he said pushing her away.

He kept his eyes directly on me as if she wasn't there. As I left the room my eyes glanced back at the wrinkled sheets on the bed that delivered the guilty verdict. "Monica, let's go I'm so over this," I said trying not to display my devastation.

Chapter Two

Before I could get in the car, Monica exploded with questions. "What the hell happened in there? What did he say? What did you say?" "Nothing much, you know the same old Sean," I failed to emphasize. "Bitch I want details; you just caught your man of eight years in bed with your cousin, who claims she has, *not one*, but four babies for him and you talked about nothing much," Monica said.

I laughed as I thought about my best friend's brutally honest personality. "Basically he said he was sorry and he would never do it again." "Bullshit," Monica interrupted. "Can I finish please," I interrupted. "Go on, this should be good."

"You won't believe when this started, remember when I flew out to LA for the reading of my parents will. Well, Sean goes over to the house and you know that's when Tasha was staying with me. He claims he brought champagne and roses to make up for his many mistakes. He lets himself in and they started drinking and talking and one thing led to another.

Oh damn, I forgot to get my keys back. Monica you have to get my keys from him. I just can't deal with that drama right now."

"You know that man is not going to give me your keys," Monica admitted. "So what am I going to do," I asked. "Just change the locks," Monica suggested. "True, I'll handle that first thing in the morning." "Just finish the story," Monica was dying to know.

"Can you believe he wanted me to leave with him tonight?" "And go where?" "Who knows? Basically he was saying forget about Tasha, the four kids and what you saw tonight and we can go on living our lives.

Monica I can't deny that I'm in love with this man. I want to be his wife and have a house full of little Sean's running around, but I know I deserve better and I have too much going for myself to be some trophy wife that he puts on the shelf to admire and dust off every now and then."

"Well good. I'm glad you finally realize that. He doesn't deserve you and he knows that, but if he really loves you he'll let you go to have that fairy tale life you had before you met him." "I've had enough of Sean for tonight, let's go to Waffle House," I suggested.

As Monica and I pulled up to Waffle House it was packed, as usual. Everybody knows Waffle House is the club after the club. There was no parking spaces insight, especially with someone's extra large hummer limo taking up so many spaces.

Slipping out of reality, I started thinking about how Sean and I traveled like that after his shows. "Angel, earth to Angel," Monica said. "Sorry girl my mind was in a totally different place." "I wonder whose rolling in the limo," Monica asked. Before entering the building we could already see there was standing room only. I was definitely not in the mood for this, but Monica insisted that we stay. As soon as we hit the door Monica recognized her-ex Kevin.

"Come on, let's go sit with Kevin," Monica said. "You sure he's not going to mind." "He doesn't have a choice," Monica replied. "What's up Kevin," spoke Monica. "What's up baby girl, what's up Angel have a seat," Kevin said. "I planned to," Monica stated. "Angel meet my cousins Paul and Tony; Monica you remember them from the family reunion in Key West," Kevin said.

Everyone shook hands and gave greetings. "Damn, Monica you're looking good; you've really been taking care of yourself. So, what's been going on? It's been about six months since I've seen you last,"

Kevin announced. "Kevin you know I'm pre law at Miami University, one more year and I will be Attorney Monica Sawyer," she said proudly. Monica was known in the hood as ghetto but please don't let her loud and over the top demeanor fool you. She and I both graduated suma cum larde and she still maintained a 4.0 at Miami University.

"I'm proud of you; I always have been." "So Angel, is Sean in town," Kevin asked. "Yeah, I think so," I replied not wanting to show any evidence that there was trouble in paradise. "Why is it so packed in here tonight," I asked. "Some big CEO of this record label in Atlanta is here and everybody's trying to bombard him with demos," Kevin announced. "He looks a bit frustrated," Monica said.

"Wouldn't you," I asked. "Just imagine being hounded everyday; someone looking for you to determine their destiny.

That's like carrying the world on your shoulders," said Paul. "I think we all can agree that we wouldn't want that pressure," Tony declared. "Is everyone ready to order," said the waitress interrupting our conversation. "Yes, I'll have the smothered hash browns hold the onions and a glass of V-8 Juice with no ice," I said. "And I'll have a chicken melt and a glass of sweet tea with no ice," Monica ordered. "We'll have three well done steak dinners and a pitcher of lemonade," said Kevin ordering for Paul and Tony as well.

After the orders were placed I found it the perfect time to excuse myself to the ladies room. Making it to the ladies room was just as hard as finding a table. Not too far from the restrooms was a small-secluded table nestled in the back surrounded by bodyguards. All of this for a record executive; the way they were acting you would have thought it was Jesus passing out miracles. "Excuse me miss but, you can't come through this way," a larger than life bodyguard spoke. "Sir this is a public place and I'm trying to get to the restroom," I said in a panic. "I've been giving strict orders not to let anyone pass. Mr. Jones does not want to be disturbed." "I don't want him to be disturbed either but I'm about to wet my clothes." "There's a gas station next door."

I could not believe what was going on. I really wasn't the type to cause a scene so I was more then nervous when the gentleman sitting at the back table came forth and whispered something in his ear. Now by this time, I'm thinking he could either physically remove me from this area or they thought I was a groupie and wanted to give me the room key to their hotel.

"Okay miss it's cool you can go through," the guard spoke. "Thank You," I exhaled. After that was over and I finally was allowed to use the restroom, I decided to check my voice messages before going back out to the chaos. Hearing in frustration the digital voice say; "You have ten new messages from Sean."

In better judgment I decided to delete them all. I definitely was dreading going back pass security. I took a deep breath and tried to walk as fast as I could until I felt a light tap on my shoulders.

"Excuse me miss, Mr. Jones would like to have a word with you," said the bodyguard. "For what," I asked. "Right this way, follow me." Before he could announce me, the gentleman that he referred to as Mr. Jones stood up and introduced himself as Charles Jones, CEO and President of Out of Control Records. "Angel Jordan, it's a pleasure to meet you. Look Mr. Jones." "Please call me Charles," he insisted. "Charles, I'm not an artist nor do I inspire to be so I'm a little confused as to why you asked me over here." "I noticed you, as you and your friend came in the door. You have a certain charm and natural beauty that's a rare find these days. If you hadn't come this way I would have eventually come to you."

"Charles I have to get back to my friends before they send out a search party for me." "Angel, I will be in town until tomorrow. Please have lunch with me, you don't have to accept now just take my card and call me when you're ready," Charles said with great hope in his eyes. "I don't think so," I said returning his card.

He hadn't been rejected like that since college and that made the chase even more exciting. "That's the one. I don't know when but she's going to be Mrs. Jones," he swore to his partners.

"Where the hell you been," Monica asked. "Being harassed!" "By who," everyone said at once. "No it's cool let's just eat," I said to downplay what I had just been through. I don't know how, but Monica knew when I was withholding information. We ate and said our goodbyes to Kevin and his crew, as we vowed to keep in touch.

As Monica pulled up in my driveway my mind was in a whirlwind about the events that had just transpired only hours ago.

"Are you spending the night Monica?" "No not unless you need me to. I have an early morning class." "Alright call me when you reach home and thanks for everything. I love you." "I love you more," Monica said as she sped off into the night.

Chapter Three

As I walked through the house everything reminded me of Sean; the fireplace, the Jacuzzi, the pool and all four of the bedrooms we christened with our passion.

It didn't help that his clothes still remained in his closet and the scent of Izzy Mikaye lingered through the house.

I knew I wasn't getting any sleep so I turned on the surround sound system that played all over the house. Prince's "Adore", Freddie Jackson and Luther Vandross. CD's Sean had put in the other night. This only would make matters worst, so I popped out our baby making CD's and promptly placed in some Lil Kim and Trina for motivation.

Before I knew it all of his clothes, his Cartier, Rolexes and his alligator Timberland collection were in boxes. I didn't know what time it was but I was exhausted and could see the sun coming up.

There's one more thing I had to do, so I reached for the yellow pages to look for a locksmith. I jotted down the number for a 24-hour service. First I needed a shower to refresh myself. Ten minutes into my shower I saw someone come in the front door from the surveillance system in the bathroom.

I knew it was Sean; he was the only one with keys and the alarm code.

"Damn, why hadn't I called the locksmith before I showered?" The door slammed behind him and he called out to me. I didn't say a word, hoping he wouldn't come upstairs and find me in the shower. You could say Sean had a problem keeping his hands to himself when I was concerned. "Angel Eyes, I'm home where are you," he yelled out. 'Is this man serious, how dare he show his face here and act like everything is all good.'

As he found his way upstairs, over the boxes and in the bathroom something inside of me wished he had found me with some other guy screwing my brains out; it would serve him just right.

"Sean, what are you doing here? We ended this last night. Get outta here, I'm in the shower," I screamed.

"It's nothing I haven't seen before," he said smiling with a devilish grin.

Before I could grab my towel and jump out he was in the shower with me with my hands penned up over my head. Sean was the first and only guy I had ever been with.

He was exploring my body like a groom on his wedding night. With every kiss he whispered, "I'm sorry I want you to have my baby."

My mind was saying stop this isn't right but, my body had a mind of its' own.

He carried me out of the shower and laid me on the bed. He turned me every which a way but loose. "Sean, we shouldn't…" "Shh just let me love you," he said with the sweetest voice I ever heard. We made love for hours.

He held me in his arms; kissing and caressing me so softly that it sent my body

into uncontrollable shakes. He begun to go down and kiss me in his secret garden; that's what he liked to call it. He swore he had never smelled a woman so fragrant or tasted a woman so sweet. Tears begin to roll down my face for I knew this was the last time I would make love to the only man that had ever known me this way. I must have slept for what felt like days because when I woke up he was gone and there was a Tiffany's box, a plane ticket and a note on the nightstand that read:

Angel Eyes,

I had to fly to NY to do tapings for MTV and BET. Enclosed is a roundtrip ticket for you to meet up with me. Last night was like making love to you for the first time. You are my life and I can't live it without you. I know I really hurt you this time and I don't deserve you but give me one last chance to make you my wife.

Love,
Sean

I read the note at least ten times, just trying to make sense of it all. The message alert on my cell phone woke me out of my daydream. 'You have three new messages from Sean.' He was the last person I wanted to call but God knows I didn't need him hopping on a plane just because he couldn't reach me. "Hi babe, what's up," I said in my what do you want now tone.

"Yo Angel I've been calling you all day." "I'm still in the bed, I'm tired," I admitted. "I know I put it on you last night," Sean boasted. He wasn't lying about that. My thighs were so sore it felt like I was the chick being passed from the bodyguard to the hype man and finally to the artist.

Last night we weren't making love to each other we were making love to our emotions. "Shut up, what do you want anyway?"

"Did you like the necklace," Sean asked. "Yes, you know Tiffany's is my favorite place," I responded.

"What time does your flight get here?" "Babe, why do I need to fly to New York? There's nothing for me to do; you'll be doing autograph signings, interviews and video shows all day."

"I have a two day itinerary and the rest of the week is yours and besides moms wants to see you," Sean explained. "Yeah, I do need to call her. My flight leaves Miami International at 8:15 and lands at LaGuardia at 10:45 tonight. I'm going to lie back down for an hour."

"I love you girl."

"Okay, I'll see you later Sean."

"Oh you can't say you love me now, you didn't have that problem last night," Sean said reminding me of what should have never happened.

"I love you too, goodbye."

My mind was made up I was leaving Miami and Sean for good.

Chapter Four

I had to call Sean back and make up an excuse as to why I wasn't coming to New York. I didn't want to tip him off because it would send him into a whirlwind. I needed some place to go, to map out my life without him.

So I called Monica to see if she could take her classes online and travel to the Bahamas with me for a few months. "I'm sure my counselor can arrange that. I'll just tell her it's an emergency," said Monica. "Perfect, I'll call my travel agent and have him make reservations for Thursday morning."

"I have tons of shopping to do," said Monica unable to contain herself. "Don't pack anything we'll do our shopping when we get there. What time are you coming over? I need to get these locks changed and take Sean's things back to his house."

"I'll call you when I'm on the way," Monica said.

"Cool, love you."

"Love you too."

My next call would be to Sean. I didn't want to disappoint him but I had to stop disappointing myself.

I picked up the phone and he answered on the second ring. "What's up ma?" "Hi baby. How's your day been," I asked. "Busy as hell." "Are you sitting down?" "What's wrong, you pregnant?" "Hell no," I confirmed. "Why it gotta be all like that; after the other night you never know." Let's hope not I thought only to myself; there were certain things you just didn't say to Sean.

"Babe, I missed my flight," I lied.

"Angel how did you miss your flight, he asked.

"I overslept I was so tired and …" He cut me off before I could dig a deeper hole for myself. "What's the next one out?" "Sean it's pointless for me to fly out for a day."

"Alright whateva, just call moms she was waiting to see you." He hung up without saying goodbye. I knew that meant he was vexed.

I decided to call his mother since that had been the second time he mentioned it to me. His sister Nicole answered the phone. She recognized my voice instantly.

"What's up Angel? Are you in town?" "No I'm not coming. I missed my flight and your brother is heated with me." "He'll be alright," she said smacking her lips.

"Where's mommy?" "Right here, she's been waiting to see you." "Let me speak with her and call me sometimes. My numbers haven't changed."

"Okay here's mommy."

"How's my baby girl?" "Fine mommy how have you been?" "Blessed baby; Nicole told me you messed your flight." "Yes ma'm and I think Sean was a little aggravated." "You know that boy is crazy about you. He could never stay mad at you." I wanted to break down and talk to her like I would have talked to my mom if she were still alive. "When are you kids gonna tie the knot and give me some grandbabies? I'm starting to give up hope on my boy." Why would she give up hope on Sean having kids, didn't she know about Tasha and her four kids.

Had Sean not mentioned it to her or his family for that matter? Why?

Was he not sure himself?

I couldn't concern myself with his mess up that was his problem.

"Don't give up hope mommy; it'll happen when the time is right. I'll try to get up there in the next two months and mommy, please call me if you need anything. I love you so much." "I love you too baby and take care of Sean for me; he looked so stressed out today," mommy said with a concerned voice. That's Tasha's job now, thinking to myself. If I could help it I never wanted to see him again and once I landed in The Bahamas I didn't have to speak to him either.

I called Fernando at World Flight Travel to book two first class flights with our travel names: Thelma Evans and Louise Jefferson.

Once that was set up I begin loading the boxes into the Suburban. Just as I loaded the last box Monica just would pull up. Monica parked her jeep and hopped in the Suburban that was full to capacity.

I loved the ride from Coconut Grove to Miami Beach not too much traffic and quick.

Sean had one of the nicest mansions on Star Island. I recognized the guard at the gate Jose; who often did garden work for both houses. "Buenos Dias Mrs. Crews," said Jose. Sean insisted that Jose call me by his last name. "Good day to you as well Jose. How's the family." "Couldn't be better," Jose responded. After law school and becoming partner at a prestigious law firm I'm buying a house out here," said Monica.

Monica was the only friend I ever allowed pass these gates. I pulled into the garage and immediately ran to the bathroom. I was running to the bathroom more frequently lately.

I went through the mail and checked the messages.

"Sean this is Tasha, where are you I haven't heard from you in three days. Call me I love you."

Next message: Tuesday, 9:45pm.

"Sean it's me Tasha, what's going on, you're not answering your cell phone? I've left you several messages. Call me; I miss you."

Next message: Wednesday, 3:15pm.

"Sean it's Tasha, it's cool if you don't want anything to do with me but, you will take care of these kids regardless. If you can't call me back; I'll do what I have to do to make sure our kids are taken care of."

Next message: Wednesday, 4:26pm.

"Mr. Crews this is Dr. King returning your call about the information you requested on paternity testing. Our office hours are Monday-Friday from 8-4:30pm or feel free to call me on my direct line at (305) 555-1632."

Monica and I both gasped at that message. "Monica, everything makes sense now. I

talked to Sean's mom today and she asked, when are you guys going to have me some grandkids?"

"You know if he had any kids his mother would be the first to know." "That's the reason he hasn't told anyone; he isn't sure and doesn't want to make a fool of himself," I said as if I'd discovered a cure for cancer. "Does this change anything," Monica asked. "This changes nothing. He's getting everything he deserves.

Explain this to me; you have a good woman at home that takes care of you mentally, physically and emotionally but, you still go out and sleep around without protection that results in yes you are the father or no you are not the father."

"Because they're greedy and lack will power. You put a naked woman in front of any man and I guarantee you he's going to cheat on his women in some form. Whether it's accepting her advances or becoming aroused," Monica said summing it up.

"Monica you know what I went through when I told him I was pregnant." "I know, I'm still upset with you," Monica confessed. "What was I to do? I felt so guilty; I was getting pressure from him, management and the label," I admitted.

"It was your body and your blessing and you shouldn't let anyone make you feel guilty about that."

"You're so right but now he's all up on me talking about he wants me to have his baby."

"Stop playing," Monica laughed.

"No I'm serious, when I called him about the flight and asked if he was sitting down; he goes are you pregnant?" "You know why," Monica said. "Why," I asked. "He wants to hold on to you; something that will bond you two together for life." "If I ever found out that I was pregnant. I still wouldn't be with him," I declared. "I'm starving; what do you guys have up in here to eat," Monica complained. "Probably nothing, Sean never goes grocery shopping." I found some veggie burgers that belonged to me because he didn't do the no meat thing. For dinner that night we munched on veggie burgers and sweet potato fries.

"You know you have to help me with these boxes," I said. "Let's do this," Monica agreed. We placed all the boxes with clothes and shoes in the guestroom and The Cartier and Rolex wrist wear were locked in the safe.

I decided to go upstairs to our room to investigate while Monica was taking a swim.

It had been months since I stayed here. Nothing had really changed except for the dozens of pictures Sean had of him and I but mostly of me.

It was strange that a father wouldn't be proud to display the pictures of his seeds. There was not one picture of the children that Tasha claimed to be his.

The phone rang again. I decided to let the answering machine pick up.

"Sean it's Tasha again. I know you're with Angel but you could still pick up the phone. You have twenty-four hours to return my calls or you'll be reading the headlines announcing: Million Dollar Rap-Star is a deadbeat dad to four young children. I'm sure the media will have a field day with that story."

This bitch is psychotic.

No matter what issues I had with Sean I was not going to let some deranged lunatic destroy everything that we had worked so hard to maintain. I called my uncle Samuel; who had a medical practice in Coral Gables.

I didn't want to put him in my business so I told him I needed the information for a friend. He gave me the numbers to an old college buddy; who owned a private paternity testing company.

I immediately called Dr. Wasabi on his cell phone. "Hello," an Asian accented voice answered the phone. "Yes, Dr. Wasabi my name is Angel Jordan and my uncle Samuel told me to call you about paternity testing," I said nervously. "Well, you've called the right person. I usually don't take these calls after hours but anything for my best friend's niece. Your uncle and I go way back. He's a great person."

"Yes he is sir."

"Let me get a few details from you before I ask you to come in."

"Oh no sir it's not for me it's for a friend whose life kinda depends on it."

"How many parents are involved," said Dr. Wasabi as his line of questioning began. "Two as far as I know."

"I'm going to need the name of the mother, the alleged father and the children."

I gave him everyone's name and prepared myself for anything else he wanted to know.

"So there are four children in question?"

"Yes."

"Is the father willing to test?"

"Yes."

"Has the mother filed for child support?"

"Not that I'm aware of."

"This should be enough to get the paperwork rolling. I can schedule an appointment for next Tuesday at 10:00am. Please make your friends aware that the fee for the DNA Test will be one hundred and fifty dollars for each child. If the mother decides to file for child support the father will be responsible for providing documentation of monetary support and the results that he receives from us will stand up in court." "That's perfect Dr. Wasabi, they will see you on Tuesday and thanks for everything."

I called Sean to relay the many messages that Tasha had left and the details about my conversation with Dr. Wasabi. "Ha Babe," I said in my sweetest voice. "What's good," as Sean kept it short.

By his tone I could tell he was still upset about me not coming to New York. "We... I mean you have a serious problem," correcting myself. "Tasha has left about fifty messages about you not answering your phone or calling her back." "At your house," Sean said with anger. "No. I'm in Miami Beach."

"So what's the problem?" "She just left another message saying you had twenty-four hours to call her or she's going to the tabloids."

"What? I'll kill that bitch."

"Sean it's not that deep."

"What do you mean it's not that deep, she's messing with my livelihood!"

"I've already thought about that so I called Uncle Sam and he gave me the number to his friend, Dr. Wasabi." "And he is?" "He does DNA testing for child support cases."

"Child Support? What's that about?"

"Babe it's nothing to worry about everything is held in strict confidence. The fee is one hundred and fifty dollars per child. If the results are determined that you are the father and she files for child support, you have to provide evidence that you are supporting the children. If you're not the father and she disputes the first test and wants the courts to do one and the results come out the same then she has to reimburse you and pay for all court costs."

"When do we go?" "I'm not going. You and Tasha have to be there next Tuesday at 10:00am."

"Baby, I'm so sorry you have to go through this." "Yeah Sean I'm sorry too."

"I don't know what I would do without you. It's because of you I'm where I am today. As soon as I get home we're going to start planning that dream wedding you've always wanted."

Little did he know there would be no wedding or us.

"I just got off the phone with moms. She told me you called today."
"I did, no matter what we go through or who you end up with I will always love her." "I'm not ending up with nobody but you. You need to buy a pregnancy test; moms had a dream about fish."
"Tell me you don't believe in that stuff." "Angel I can feel it, just like the last time. When I get home I'm taking you to the doctor."
"Whateva man."
"Why are you out in Star Island? I thought you were scared to stay there by yourself." "Monica's here with me."
"Tell her I said what's up; if she's speaking to me this week." "I'll talk to you later." "Why are you rushing me off the phone," Sean inquired. "So you can handle your business with Tasha." "I'm not trying to deal with that girl right now." "It's not like you have a choice." "I picked up a little something for you to wear for me when I get home." "Later man."
When I hung up he immediately made that dreaded call to Tasha.
Tasha answered on the first ring.
"Sean."
"Bitch don't ever call my house and threaten me about no tabloids."
"Sean, I'm sorry but I was upset. I've been calling you for days. You haven't checked on the kids in three days. They have been asking about you. They need you as much as I do. I didn't make these babies by myself and I shouldn't have to take care of them by myself."

"Tasha you knew what it was when we laid down together. My intentions were never to leave Angel under any circumstances."

"It's different now I have your kids not her and what about you doing the right thing by us and marrying me," Tasha vented.

"Angel and I have a bond that not even you having kids by me can break. Kids won't tie us together if I don't love you," Sean admitted.

"Sean I don't wanna hear that."

"Tasha, I'm going to ask you one last time. Are you sure I'm the father?"

"Why are you doubting me?"

"If I find out otherwise it's gonna be hell to pay. I'm coming to get you and the kids on Tuesday. I need you to have them ready by 9:00 in the morning."

"Why?"

"Just be ready," Sean demanded.

It was getting late and we had an early morning flight so I ventured into my closet for the last time. I thought about taking my collection of Manolo Blahniks and Marc Jacobs footwear. I left everything including the five-carat Tiffany's Diamond Ring that was purchased two years prior.

Monica thought I was crazy. "Let me take it," she said. I don't want anything to remind me of him. I need a fresh start. I decided to leave him a letter.

I owed him that much.

I placed the letter along with the ring in the middle of the bed and said good-bye to Star Island.

Chapter Five

The drive back home was quiet between Monica and I.

We were both worn out and anticipating our vacation to the Bahamas.

I tossed and turned all night wrestling with my decision to leave. I prayed to God he didn't try to surprise me by leaving New York a day earlier and we ended up running into each other at the airport. How would I explain myself? I would lose all nerves if I had to tell him face to face. The alarm woke us up at six a.m.

"Today is the day I start my new life," I said.

"No second thoughts," Monica asked.

"Nope, I'll call the cab now so we won't be late," I replied.

We arrived at Miami International Airport on time and went straight to the gate since we had no baggage to check in. We were up and out of the air in no time. Monica and I were equally excited. It was our first time in Freeport. It was beautiful and I felt a sense of independence. My uncle owned a condo there and agreed to let me stay as long as I needed. I was anxious to see our living arrangements, so we grabbed a taxi to our beachfront condo.

It was immaculate; marble everywhere, Versace Furniture and thick hand made window treatments. I definitely felt at home. The first place we hit was Port Lucaya. We shopped all day until we realized we had not eaten since last night. We dropped all of our bags off at the condo and went to the seafood stand we had passed coming in.

We bought fresh lobsters, shrimp and conch for our very own seafood feast. We showered, put on our matching robes and ate lobster and conch fritters on the balcony overlooking the ocean.

"I'm so happy you agreed to come with me, there's no one else I would rather enjoy this with," I revealed. "Likewise, what are we doing tonight," Monica asked. "Let's go to a club. I bet Bahamians really know how to party," I implied. "You want to go clubbing? You never club." "I'm a single woman now. There's no one to stop me. A new life means new beginnings," I said. "Call the concierge and find out the hot spots," Monica suggested. The concierge suggested that we check out Pure Nightlife. I dressed in a black Dolce and Gabana sundress with the matching sandals and Monica wore the same expect hers was of a red floral design.

The line was wrapped around the corner. When we finally got in, the club was packed wall to wall.

"Excuse me miss, would ya like ta dance," a beautiful Hershey's chocolate man with dreads flowing down his spine asked. I looked for Monica but she had her own thing going on. "Sure, why not," I accepted.

He held me so close that I could smell Black, Kenneth Cole Cologne. This was the first time another man held me this close that it felt sinful.

"My name is Gene, ya dance very well."

"My name is Thelma."

There was no way I was giving this stranger any information about myself.

"It was a pleasure dancing with ya and until we meet again beautiful, take care."

I was relieved that he didn't ask for my number. I never did like a guy that was too pushy. It was a complete turn off.

"Where did you get lost at," I asked Monica. "I was on the balcony. I met this guy who owns the biggest law firm down here and he wants me to come by the office next week. He might have an internship available."

"Who was that fine guy you were dancing with," Monica asked.

"His name was Gene." "Did you give him the digits?" "He didn't ask," I admitted. "You wouldn't have given them away if he had." "You know me so well," I said.

"You ready to go," Monica asked. "Not really. I can't remember when I've had this much fun." We ended up closing the club down and didn't get home until four o'clock in the morning. We were beyond tired. We had been moving non-stop since we landed. I would sleep in all day tomorrow.

Monica woke up about one in the afternoon and found her way to my room. "Wake up sleepy head. Let's go sight seeing." "I can't move. Do you want me to call you a tour guide?" "No, I'll have the concierge call one for me." "Okay be safe," I said as I rolled over and went back to sleep.

Sean landed in Miami mid afternoon. His first call was to me. 'You've reached

Angel; leave a message at the tone.'

'Beep.'

"Babe I just landed. Call me when you get this message."

Sean arrived in Miami Beach later that evening. He would be in for the surprise of his life once he opened the door to his eight-bedroom mansion.

As he walked upstairs to the bedroom he noticed a letter and my ring on the bed. His heart started to pound even before he read it. He sat on the bed staring at the letter thinking that whatever was in the envelope couldn't be good. He slowly opened the letter and began to read it with panic.

Sean,

You are the only man I have ever loved. You were my first love and in more ways than one. It seems like yesterday you were begging my father to take me out. You swore to him that you would make me your wife. That's the same night you vowed to never hurt me.

Things haven't quite worked out that way. That night I found you in bed with Tasha, my heart broke into unfixable pieces.

I'm sure this wasn't the first woman just the first time you got caught. I have to end this relationship. I can't go on wondering what I'll have to deal with next. The best option for me is to leave Miami. I can't risk bumping into you or our friends; my heart will never heal. There's too much of us here. I know you will but, please don't try and find me.

Good luck with Tasha and the kids; you will make a wonderful father. If we never speak again live life to the absolute fullest and be happy with the memories I left you.

Your Love,
Angel

He fell to his knees and sobbed like a baby.
He had no one to blame but himself for messing up the best thing to come into his life.

He tried calling me again but my voicemail picked up. 'Beep.'
"Babe, please don't do this to us; we can work this out. I love you."
He made three more attempts before driving to Coconut Grove. He figured there had to be some evidence of where I had gone.

When he arrived; to his surprise the locks were changed. He was feeling every emotion possible; anger, hurt and guilt. He called every airline but they all gave him the same line. "Sorry, we can't give out that information sir."

His last result was Monica. "Hello," Monica answered not recognizing the number. "Yo Monica it's Sean. What the hell is going on?"

"What are you talking about?"

"Where's Angel? I'm going out of my mind. She left me this letter that had a nigga crying like a baby. She even left the ring; she never takes that ring off," Sean vented.

"I don't know where she is and if I did I wouldn't tell you."

"Monica, I swear to God I will spend every dollar I have to find her."

"Why? She's moving on let her be happy. Put yourself in her shoes. Can you imagine what she's feeling right now?"

"I've changed, that's behind me," Sean confessed.

"In five days, you've changed," Monica said sarcastically. "If you talk to her just have her call me. I can't even sleep in this house, knowing she's gone. Why didn't she take anything; her clothes, shoes, Louis Vuitton luggage, Coach Bags and all of her diamonds?"

"Sean you of all people should know Angel has never been about material things. Every woman you had flings with wanted something from you. For heaven's sake you were high school sweethearts. She was there before the money and fame; you should have shown her more respect," Monica said in a rage. "You're absolutely right but, I'm trying to be that man right now," Sean explained. "I think it's a little too late for that." "Just have her call; I need to know if she's alright," Sean said with concern. "I'm sure she's fine but, I'll tell her if I speak with her," Monica promised.

Before returning home Monica stopped by the seafood stand to pick up two fresh lobsters for dinner.

"Angel you up yet," Monica yelled. "I'm in the tub," I yelled back. Monica put the lobsters on ice and ran upstairs to unload the conversation she had with Sean. When she opened the door I was submerged in bubbles and surrounded by hazelnut scented candles. Monica sat on the edge of the big-jetted tub. "You will not believe who I've been talking to for the past hour," Monica said.

"Who," I asked. "Sean," Monica confessed.

"Stop lying," I said. "He said he has left you several messages. He went by your house and called all the airlines. He's turned into a mad man; it's rather pathetic. He starting crying about some letter you wrote. What was in that letter," Monica asked.

"Something I should have said years ago," I admitted.

"So what are you going to do? He said he would spend every dollar to find you." "Why is he doing this? Why won't he just let me go?" "When a determined man wants something bad enough he won't stop until he gets it."

"I'm not calling him. I'm done and I mean it." "I hope you stick to your guns this time."

"Are we going out to dinner," I asked. "No, I picked up lobsters and I can make a shrimp salad," Monica offered.

"I'll be down in a minute."

34

I finished my bath; put my robe on and went downstairs to find a movie for dinner.

"How did you enjoy your tour of the island?" "This place is like being in paradise. The water is so clear you can see the fish swimming. I'm falling in love with this place." "Me too," I admitted.

"When do your online classes start?" "Monday," Monica said in a dreadful voice. "Let's go to Paradise Island for the weekend," I suggested. "You know I'm down." We finished our dinner put on a movie and fell asleep to the sounds of Sophia threatening to kill Harpo died.

When we awoke it was a new day. I dreaded checking my messages. I already knew what the deal was. Monica had the concierge call us a cab before we arrived downstairs. We dressed and picked up sun hats because the sun was already tanning our peanut butter skin. I had heard such great things about Paradise Island that my anticipation was uncontainable. Monica's phone rang.

"It's Sean," she whispered.

I rolled my eyes in annoyance.

"Hello," Monica answered the phone trying not to laugh at my facial expression. "Monica what's up? Have you heard from her yet?"

"Yes."

"Where is she?"

"She didn't say."

"You didn't ask?"

"That's not my job, if she wanted you to know she would have informed you." It took everything inside of him not to cuss her out.

He was not in the mood for her smart mouth today. He had to keep his cool because she was his only link to me. "Sean I don't know how else to say this but, she said it's over. She wants nothing else to do with you." "How can she just walk away like that?" "That's something you have to ask her." "Just tell her I love you." "Bye Sean." "What did he say," I asked.

"Look, you need to call him; it's not going to be too many times that I play the messenger."

"I'll buy a phone card and call him when we return on Sunday."
"He needs to hear it from your mouth that it's over."

"For now let's just lose ourselves in the magic of this place," I suggested. We partied and shopped all weekend long. We even managed to play a little golf. I bought Sean's mother and sister three tropical outfits with the gemstone sandals to match and tons of postcards to present to them on my trip to New York next month. Monica and I were happy to be back in Freeport. I had the driver stop me at the corner store to buy a phone card.

I knew how Sean would blow up my phone if I were unreachable, so I could only imagine what Monica was going through. I went upstairs to my room and closed the door behind me and prepared to call Sean.

"Angel," Sean answered as if he were waiting for my call. "Sean," I said nervously. "Where are you and what's going on?"

"I can't tell you that. You know what's going on. Didn't you read the letter?" "Yeah, I read the letter but you had to do it like that?"
"That was the best way for me." "What about the other night? I thought we made up." "Why would you think that, because we slept together?"

"Yeah."

"You practically raped me."

"I raped you?"

"I didn't say you raped me I said practically. As I recall I was in the shower and you jumped in with me pulling me out and penning me down on the bed until I let you have your way."

"Not once did I hear you tell me to stop."

I said nothing trying to think of a come back. "I'm not having this conversation on the phone. Where are you? I'm getting ready to catch a flight out to you." "Sean that's my point; there's no conversation to have. I just can't take anymore. I'm done!"

"You're just going to throw eight years away," Sean asked. "You did," I lashed back.

"I want only you and I'm not resting until you're mine again. What am I suppose to do with this big ass house. I bought this for you." "I can't answer that but you have to let me go. I can't pretend I'm happy when I'm not." "You saying you don't love a nigga no more." "That's not what I'm saying. I will always love you; I just don't trust you." "I know it's gonna take time to build that trust up again but can't you give me another chance to prove myself to you." "You wrote the lyrics to your own song. You're making this harder than it already is. You can't keep blowing up everybody's phone especially mine. I need my space." "Is space all you need? Cool. Have your space, get your thoughts together and then come back home." "Have you not heard a word I said? I'm not coming home." "All right. Whatever. Promise me you'll go check on my baby," Sean said catching me off guard. "What baby," I asked. "My baby you're carrying."

"A baby is not going to bring me home." "Don't make me come get you," Sean said with his rude boy attitude. "Good night," I said trying to hang up the phone. "I love you so much; you don't even know." "I love," I caught myself before I reciprocated the feelings. "You don't have to play the hard role. I know you love me." I quickly hung up the phone to regain my composure before going downstairs with Monica. "How did it go," Monica asked. She knew something was wrong with me. No matter how hard I tried to fight the tears they came anyway. "Why is he making this so hard? I just want to go on with my life." "Sweetie you have to realize it's only been a few days and you all have been together since high school. Nothing happens overnight. It's going to take time for both of you to heal and get over this."

"He doesn't see it that way. After all the dirt he has done on the road and now this Tasha situation; he really expects things to be the same.

I was stupid for him and it's not good when a woman is stupid over a man; you lose who you are and everything you stand for. I could've seen him all up and through a female and if he'd said 'it wasn't me' my mind would start second guessing itself like maybe it wasn't him." "That's not stupid that's retarded," Monica said laughing. "First loves are always the hardest to get out of your system."

"I don't believe in any of those first love myths. It's like this, if you let a man get away with something once he's gonna continue to do it just because he knows he can. You put up with a lot of his bullshit. It's just like when you flew out to Japan to surprise him and he was missing in action and Tommy had to keep you company the whole time you were there. Sean was already getting enough you should have put it on Tommy's ass." "Monica their damn near brothers, that would be breaking the code," I said with my mouth wide open shocked by her suggestion. "He threw the code out the window when he slept with Tasha, all's fair in love and war."

"It's still not right." "You are a good one because he would have been dropped like hotcakes years ago," Monica said. "When you decide to be with someone in this business; you're with them, the industry and what comes along with it," I said. "That's exactly why I could never date a rapper," Monica confessed. "All rap artists are not that way." "No thank you. Lawyers and Doctors applications accepted only." "You're crazy,"

I said managing a smile. "Sean thinks I'm pregnant." "He thinks what?" "He thinks I'm pregnant and wants me to go get checked out." "So he's a doctor now. How did he come to that diagnosis?" "He says he just feels it." "What do you feel; are you going to check it out," Monica asked. "I'm not sure I want to know. That would be too much to inhale right now," I admitted. "Just don't wait too long; if not for Sean just for your piece of mind." Monica and I stayed up all night gossiping about our celebrity friends and pigging out on every junk food created. Before we knew it Sunday had come and gone. The continuous ring of my cellular phone awakened me. "Angel Eyes, I need you. I didn't sleep all night." "Sean I'm not doing this today." "I need to hold you," Sean begged.

"Tasha's there, hold her." "I'm not saying I was right but what I had with her was strictly sex but I make love to you and only you." "You're right, it wasn't right and now you have to suffer the consequences and live with it." "I can't live with it; I refuse to. I had a show in L.A. last night but I was too sick to go." "What's wrong with you," I asked. "I can't eat or sleep." "Baby you're not sick you're just going through withdraws." "I know that's why I'm sending the jet to pick you up now." "Man take that somewhere else; I'm out."

I hung up the phone and decided to go down to the beach for a swim. The sun was extremely hot so I took a number along side everyone else sipping pina coladas under the cabana. "Thelma," a deep accented voice asked unsure of himself. It took me a moment to turn around; forgetting the name I was going by. "Thelma it's me, Gene." "Gene," I said nonchalantly as if I could forget someone as beautiful as this.

"Remember me from the club the other night," he said trying to help my memory. "Oh yeah it's good to see you again." "Finding ya way through the island alright," Gene wondered. "Not really but, I'm going to jump on one of those tour buses." "Why don't ya let a native show ya around," he suggested. "Sure, why not." "How does tomorrow sound," he asked. "Tomorrow at noon; same spot," I confirmed. "Can't wait," he said with too much excitement. I hope I didn't just hook up with a psycho.

The sun was still too hot so I sat in on a yoga class. It was my first yoga experience and I was surprised how refreshed I felt from the drama that had been clouding around me. I made it official and signed up for the Monday and Thursday classes.

I could see the sun coming down from the horizon. I placed my towel on the sand, took off my top, lay on my stomach and let the noise and smell of the ocean take me away. In my subconscious mind, images of Sean dressed in a black tux and me in a white diamond encrusted Vera Wang Wedding Dress with kids running and jumping on us yelling "mommy" and "daddy" seemed so close to my touch but was too far to hold. I couldn't help but wonder what tomorrow would hold for Sean and Tasha. There was a part of me that wanted him not to be the father because I always wanted to be the woman to give him his first child and the other part wished they were for Tasha's sake. If the tests came out any other way she wouldn't live to tell about it.

"Excuse me ma'm there's no sleeping on the beach." I immediately jumped up along with my exposed breasts. Monica burst out laughing. "You should have seen the look on your face." "You're evil. I'm gonna get you for that one," I vowed. "Have you been laid out all day?" "No. I had an interesting day. I went to my first yoga class." "How was it," Monica asked. "Exhilarating.

I signed up for Monday and Thursday classes, you should come with me." "Maybe, I have so much work to do." "That's exactly why you need to do it," I explained. Although I put law school on hold to tour the seven continents with Sean; I still managed to study so I offered to help Monica with her work to free up her time. "I almost forgot. Remember the guy I danced with at the club?" "Yeah."
"Well I ran into him today. He's taking me sight seeing tomorrow." "Good, you need someone to help you forget about you know who."

"Speaking of you know who, he takes his paternity tests tomorrow." "Are you going to call him," Monica asked. "No. I'm sure he'll call and tell me all about it." "I would love to be a fly on that wall," Monica confessed. We both laughed.

Chapter Six

Sean reached Tasha's apartment promptly at nine o'clock. He had the concierge call upstairs. There was no answer so he called from his cell phone. "Hello," Tasha answered in her sexiest octave. "I'm downstairs," Sean said in his most aggravated baritone. "Come up," Tasha begged. "Hell no," Sean disconnected the conversation. By the tone of his voice Tasha knew he was a storm to be reckoned with. In minutes Tasha and the kids were packed in the Escalade. Unsuspecting to her, she was on her way to find out what was really real. "You look extra fine this morning." "Thanks," Sean replied. "I missed you baby. I haven't seen you in weeks. I knew you couldn't stay away from this," Tasha said sure of herself. "Is that right," Sean chuckled. "Fo sho, you know Angel ain't working that right. If she was you wouldn't be messing with me."

"Angel and I have never had a problem in the bedroom. I'm sure she can teach you a few things." "If it's like that; why are you here with me," Tasha asked looking for the right answer. "I've been asking myself the same question. I don't know what the hell I was thinking." "Forget you punk. Where are we going anyway?"

"You'll see when we get there; we'll be there soon." "You better not be trying to kidnap me because I told Roxanne I was with you." "Bitch don't sweat yourself." Sean pulled up in front of the doctor's office but Tasha was too busy stunt'n in Sean's truck to notice they had stopped. "We're here, get out." "What's this?" "The doctor's office." "What's this all about, you got something," Tasha said in a panic.

"All of us are taking paternity tests today." "What are you talking about we're taking paternity tests? You punk ass nigga I didn't agree to this. We ain't taking nothing. Who put you up to this; Angel?" "She had nothing to do with this." "Bullshit! This has her name written all over it. I know she put you up to this."

"When I get these kids out of this truck; you better not be too far behind." She jumped out following Sean and the kids.

Once Sean settled the kids, he took a deep breath and signed in. "S. Crews you can go ahead to the back, your paperwork was already done," the nurse said from behind the window. Sean said a prayer before he went back.

"Dear Lord, whatever the outcome of these tests please let me be able to handle the results like a man."

The tests were over in no time and the doctor explained they would receive the results by mail in two weeks. Tasha was still upset that Sean kept this from her so she insisted on taking a cab home. "Cool, here's fifty for you to take a cab but, I'll drop the kids by your moms." "You're not taking my kids anyway." "Oh, their your kids now?" "Sean you really hurt me. It's like you don't trust me." "I don't. Come on Tash, you and I both know I wasn't the only guy you were sleeping with." "You were. You don't get it. I'm in love with you and only you."

"Why would you allow yourself to fall in love with me when you knew and understood my relationship with Angel?" "Wasn't it you that said we were getting married. You know it's easier for women to get emotional attached but, for most of you men you don't have to feel anything for the woman to sleep with her." "Now that's the first truth I've heard from you all day," Sean agreed.

"Alright, we'll see you later." "Where are you going? You're just going to leave me in the middle of nowhere?" "I thought you were taking a cab." "I changed my mind. I at least have that right. Don't I?" "Whatever you wanna do man, just get in so we can bounce."

Tasha hopped in the front seat and for a moment pretended that everything was perfect. She was with the man she craved and her secret weapons that would tie them together for life. "Have the kids eaten," Sean asked. "No." Sean almost suggested South Beach. He remembered that was Angel's territory. Being seen with Tasha there would be like sleeping with Tasha in their bed; something you just didn't do. Sean stopped at The Seafood Restaurant on 103rd and let everyone order to their hearts desire. Tasha ordered a three pound lobster for herself and popcorn shrimp for the kids.

"How are you gonna order first class and the kids are riding coach. The kids are always first class, especially when I'm around. Order them all lobsters." Tasha was grinning from ear to ear. She loved how Sean balled out of control like money wasn't an issue. She had never been with someone so generous and confident of whom he was. He had a certain swagger that was magnetic and he knew it. Tasha was so turned on that she imagined herself throwing everything off the table and giving Sean his dessert before the main course.

"What's wrong with you? Why are you starring at me like that," Sean asked. "I'm hot. I want you," Tasha said in a whisper. "Oh good, here comes the food," said Sean quickly shutting that idea down. "Sir would you like refills on their drinks," the waitress asked. "Their fine for now, just bring more napkins please," Sean responded. "Sure sir, I'll be right back. Will there be anything else." "Not now, we're cool for now," Sean answered. "Sean you didn't respond. I want you now." "Tash give it a rest, just eat."

"Here you are sir," said the waitress politely laying the napkins on the table. "You have very beautiful and well behaved children," the waitress added. "Uh-Um," Tasha said clearing her throat. "You do see me sitting here right." "I'm sorry ma'am. I meant no disrespect." "I'm sure, they never do." "If you guys need anything else my name is Renee."

"Do you act a fool everywhere you go," Sean asked. "No. She saw me sitting here with you and never looked my way or addressed me at all." "I thought she was rather nice." "I'm sure you did." "Call it women's intuition; I know when a female is up to something." "Like you were with me?" "Exactly."

"Do you think Angel knew about us before that night at Todd's house?" "No. She always tries to see the good in people." That was a sword to Sean's heart to hear that. "She's the sweetest person I know and I hate that we did this to her but, what's done is did and we can't cry about it now," Tasha explained.

"I love that girl so much. I can't lose her behind this bullshit." "What about me?" "Don't worry about that. I'll make sure you and the kids are taken care of, if the kids are mine." "If," Tasha interrupted.

"I'm just saying. If they are mine I want them to come live with me and

Angel." "I'm not down with that. I will not have my kids calling another woman mommy when I'm the one who went through the pains." "It was just a suggestion." "A bad one I might add." "Angel loves children; she would be a good step mom." "I do not doubt that. I just don't want her to end up hating my kids for

45

not being hers." "I'll make sure she has plenty of her own babies." Tasha rolled her eyes and excused her self to accompany the kids to the restroom.

Renee saw the perfect opportunity to approach Sean. "Sir is your wife finished with her plate." "She's not my wife and I think she is." "I'm sorry. I hope I didn't offend you." "No. It's cool." "I hope I'm not being to direct or stepping out of my place but I find you very attractive and I would love the chance to get to know you."

Renee slid her number to Sean and finished clearing the table. 'Tasha was right damn that women's intuition,' he thought to himself. Sean politely took the number knowing he would trash it as soon as he left. He didn't need any more problems. His only focuses were the outcome of the tests and getting Angel back. Tasha and the kids finally emerged from the restroom.

"You kids ready to go," Sean asked. "Yes," they all chanted together. Sean left a hundred dollar tip on the table. "A hundred dollars; what does she need a hundred dollars for? The service wasn't even that great," Tasha complained. "Most waitresses are college students or aspiring models and every little bit helps the struggle." "Can we stop by the mall," Tasha asked. "For the kids?" "No. I need to pick up a few things for myself." "I have a flight to catch; I don't have time."

When Sean pulled up to Tasha's apartment all of the children were laid out in a deep sleep. Against his gut feelings, he decided to help Tasha carry them in. After he laid each one down, tucked them into bed and kissed them good-bye he wondered if the kids he was falling in love with were really his. He walked out to the living room but Tasha was still in the back. "Tasha, I'm out," he yelled.

Tasha ran out the back as exposed as the day she was born. She threw herself on him and began sucking on his neck. "I've been wanting you all day and you're gonna give me what I want," Tasha demanded. He immediately pushed her to the ground. She didn't look the same in his eyes anymore; all he could see was Angel. "Shorty, slow your roll. I'm done with that." "Sean. Baby, it's me Tash. I'm standing here with no clothes on and you're not all over me."

"Go put some clothes on before my kids walk out and see you like this," he said in disgust. "When are you coming back," Tasha asked wanting to cry. "I'm not sure. My schedule is full for the next month." Just like that he left Tasha standing naked on the other side of the door. Tasha got dressed and called her best friend Roxanne; formally known as Ricky. Roxanne was a transgender flier than most real women; standing five nine with a coke bottle shape that not even the finest plastic surgeon could duplicate.

"Talk to me girl," Roxanne said answering the phone. "What's up girl," Tasha asked. "Shit," Roxanne replied. "I'm so depressed." "Why? What happened with Sean this morning?" "You will not believe where this asshole took me." "Where girl?" "To get paternity tests done." "Oh no that nigga didn't girl! You didn't take it? Did You?" "Yes. I had no other choice."

"Did you tell him that you were sleeping with Andre and there's a chance that he could be the father as well?" "Are you loco? Why would I tell him that? I know when I got pregnant and there's no way they could be Dre's kids." "You better hope; better yet you better pray not." "I know right," Tasha agreed. "When was the last time you talked to Dre anyway," Roxanne asked.

"He was over here yesterday trying to push up on it." "You still sleeping with him?" "I did yesterday; a sistas got needs. I can't sit around here waiting for Sean's indecisive ass." "When was the last time you slept with Sean?" "Three weeks ago when all of this drama went down." "I heard Angel beat you down," Roxanne noted, unable to control her laughter. "You're suppose to be my girl." "I am but the shit's funny. You know she had every right to do what she did. I told you never to get involved with him in the first place. Bitches will kill you these days for messing with their man." "Sean and I were talking about that today. I know I crossed the line but, I'm in love with him."

"In love," Roxanne said shocked to hear the news flash. "I've fallen in love with this man. No one has ever treated me like he does." "You mean no one has ever spent money on you like he does." "It's not about the money anymore," Tasha confessed. "You need to snap out of it girlfriend.

He is obsessed with Angel and what you or any other woman has between her legs is not going to change that." "Seriously, I know he doesn't love me. I can feel it when he touches me. He has never made love to me it's strictly lust. He doesn't even like to kiss or hold me.

I'm never the one that's by his side at those award shows, movie premieres or who he flies around the country in private jets. Hell, we have never been outside of Miami together." "That's why you have to let him go; this isn't a healthy relationship." "How do you let go of someone that you've scheduled your whole world around and not to mention have four kids by?" "So you're saying all you're worth is a piece of ass." "No. Roxanne come on be real now." "I am being real girl. How you portray yourself to a man is how he will treat you. If you act like a slut he'll treat you like a slut. That's exactly how Sean treats you. Have you ever met his parents or been to that larger than P. Diddy's bank account mansion I heard he got." "No but that was until we told Angel," Tasha explained.

"But nothing. When a man has never taken you to his house or you can only call his cell phone then you best believe there's a wifey on the other side that he's protecting. You need to go back to cosmetology school and do something for yourself. You's a bad girl when it comes to hair; maybe Sean could hook you up with some of his celebrity friends," Roxanne suggested.

There was no denying that Tasha was the baddest bitch when it came to hair and make-up. "I would love to go back to school but I don't have the money and who's going to watch all of these kids." "I'm sure Sean would help you with the money." "I'm sure he would," Tasha agreed.

"So what's up for tonight," Roxanne asked. "I wanna hit this new club on South Beach. I heard LL is gonna be there," Tasha announced. "Are you going," Roxanne asked. "I'll go if you go," Tasha said. "For LL, why wouldn't I be there?"

"Meet me here at ten o'clock." "Wait. What are you wearing," Roxanne asked. "I'll probably wear the black halter top dress I picked up last week at Macy's," Tasha replied. "Okay girl; I'll see you tonight."

Tasha began flipping through the pages of her babysitters address book. She called Tracy and Lisa but they declined because they both were going to see LL Cool J too. Her last resort was her mother. She did not feel like hearing the lecture about how she was a mother of four and it was time out for running the streets. Tasha thought what the hell and called her anyway.

"Hi mommy." "Ha baby, how are my grandbabies doing?" "Their fine, we just put them down for their naps." "We," Tasha's mother asked. "Sean and I," Tasha responded. "I see you still haven't learned your lesson from messing with that boy." "No mommy, we had a doctor's appointment today and the kids are just tired from waking up so early," Tasha explained. "Is everything alright?" "Yes ma'am everything's fine. Sean wanted a paternity test." "Tasha I told you this day would come. What did Angel say about it?" "I haven't talked to her and who cares what she has to say about it."

"Hold on now baby, despite the circumstances you two are still family. God bless my sista's soul. Your auntie must be turning over in her grave right now about how you and Angel are carrying on. Sweet Angel; I can only imagine what that poor child is going through. Ya'll both need to leave that good for nothing boy alone," Tasha's mother raved. "Poor Angel, why does it always have to be about her? Angel is far from poor. She has the heart and love of the man I have always dreamed about and she has more money than she could spend in ten life times," Tasha acknowledged. "Money don't make you happy baby."

"I know mommy but I didn't call for all of that. Can you watch the kids for me tonight?" "Sure baby; I would love to see my grands. Pack their pajamas and an extra pair of clothes. I'll bring them home sometime tomorrow." Tasha could not believe she got a yes without a lecture. "Thanks mommy I'll see you in an hour." Tasha hung up from one call to make another. "Sean it's me

Tasha." "Yeah what's up shorty?" "I've been thinking." "Tash I told you earlier we are done. Finito." "It's not about that. I wanna go back to cosmetology school and I was wondering if you would help me pay for it."

"How much is it gonna cost me," Sean asked. "I don't know yet." "Call my assistant with the details and I'll have him mail the check directly to the school." "One more thing," Tasha said. "What's that," Sean asked. "What are we going to do about the kids?" "Find out how much a nanny is going to cost or I could pay your mother; either way let me know. I gotta run and catch this flight." "Thanks Sean you don't know what this means to me." "Everybody knows you got skills. If I didn't believe in you I would not waste my money."

Tasha chose The Miami Beauty School to attend for the fall. "It's a good day at The Miami Beauty School. How may I direct your call," a chipper voice answered on the other end. "Yes, I'm inquiring about your school fees and schedules for the fall." "It is a twelve month program and the next class starts on the thirteenth of August. Prices for the cosmetology classes are twelve thousand dollars; that includes your books and kit. Would you like to schedule an appointment to tour our facility and meet the instructors?" "How soon could you fit me in," Tasha asked. "How does tomorrow at nine o'clock sound," the receptionist asked. "It sounds great," Tasha said unable to imprison her excitement. "Oh, wonderful; the school will be in full force by this time and it will be easier for you to decide if this is the right school for you." "And who should I ask for." "You can ask for me, Mrs. Anderson." Tasha already knew this was the best school for her.

The Miami Beauty School was one of the top schools in the country whose

graduates were in high demand by the fashion, film and entertainment industry. Tasha called Tommy, Sean's assistant. Tommy was Sean's boy since their diaper days and was the only person besides me that he trusted.

"Sean Crew's office this is Tommy how may I assist you." "What's up Tommy; listen at you trying to sound all professional." "What cha talking about girl. I am professional we're running a multi million dollar business here." "Sean told me to call you with my school's information." "Hold on, let me grab a pen. Alright go ahead," Tommy said. "Make the check out to The Miami Beauty School for twelve thousand dollars."

"What's the address and contact information," Tommy asked. "The address is 37951 NW 75th Ave., Miami, Fl 33144. You can attention it to Mrs. Anderson at (305) 555-5555." "That should be everything I need but, if I have anymore questions I'll give you a call." "When are you sending it out?" "I'll send it Fed Ex overnight, it should be there by nine in the morning."

"Thanks Tommy I really appreciate this." "No problem, just don't forget the little people when you blow up." "Tommy you know I'm hood wit it to the day I die. Forget is not even in my vocabulary." "That's what they all say," Tommy reminded her. "You're right they do all say that. What people neglect to tell you is that when you come into money everything around you changes; associates, friends, family and your address forcing you to change," Tasha said in her justifications for forgetting where you came from.

"Now that's some real knowledge. I gotta run baby girl my BlackBerry is blowing up." "Cool. I'll see you around," Tasha said. Tasha called everyone she knew and told them how Sean was putting her through school and had hired a nanny from London to care for the kids. Tasha hadn't seen or heard from me in weeks so she was unsure if I had forgiven Sean and we were back in our honeymoon stage. She thought once I got news of this it would be only a matter of time before Sean was running back to her.

Tasha dropped the kids by her mom's place and stopped by Sue's Nail. Just as Tasha begin her spa manicure and pedicure in walked the mouth of the south Lola, sitting directly beside her. "What's up mama long time no see," Lola spoke. "Still the same old drama," Tasha admitted. "So you and Sean still kickin it," Lola asked. "No, he's too busy chasing Angel." "Chasing Angel," Lola asked as if this information was hot of the press. "Yeah girl, he said what we had was over and he was going to work it out with her."

"You must not have heard," Lola said. "Heard what," Tasha inquired. "Angel left him about a month ago." Tasha jumped up to the edge of her seat astonished by Lola words. "Details; I want all the details and don't leave anything out." "I heard she left Miami, moved all of Sean's things out of her house and changed the locks.

I heard he's going out of his mind trying to find her," Lola reported. "Where did she go," Tasha asked. "Nobody knows; not even me," Lola announced. "Thanks for the info girl, but I gotta bounce. Roxanne and I are going to see LL tonight". "Let me know if you find out anything about Angel," Lola insisted.

Lola didn't only need this information for her gossip report but she was honestly concerned. Lola and I were really close until my parents died and I cut everyone off except Monica and Sean. 'Now with Sean and I being out of her life, it's sad to think of her only having Monica to lean on,' Tasha said to herself. Tasha fought with the idea of finding me to apologize and make a mends but, guilt and shame kept her away. If she did speak with me what would she say and how would she explain the affair with Sean. Being noble had to be put on the back burner because Roxanne was already waiting at Tasha's apartment when she arrived.

"It's about time you got here," Roxanne said. "Sorry girl you been waiting long?" "Nah, I just got here. Where you been anyway?" "I stopped by Sue's to get my nails done and ran into Lola," Tasha explained. "Whose business was she spreading today?" "I actually enjoyed our conversation today. She told me a lot of things that I had no clue about." "And that would be," said Roxanne expecting Tasha to expand on her statement. "She said Angel left Sean and nobody knows where she is." "Oh yeah," Roxanne said. "You don't look surprised. Did you already know about this?"

"Everybody knew about it." "Well I didn't; damn Roxanne why didn't you tell me?" "What difference would it have made?" "Who gives a damn what difference it would have made. You're supposed to have my back in every situation and you keep something like this from me," Tasha flipped.

"It was for your own good. What is it going to take for you to realize that this man doesn't want you? Sean is Angel's man and always will be no matter whom he ends up with. She lives inside his head and you can't compete with that."

"I'm not trying to compete with her but I deserve to be happy."

"You do deserve to be happy but, not with your cousin's man. You can't tell me you don't see anything wrong with this." "At first I thought it was wrong; but it grew into something beautiful. Don't you think I want to move on with someone else?" "Actions speak louder than words." "What do you expect me to do he's the father of my children. It will never be me without him." "You know I love you and I just want you to be happy," Roxanne confessed. "I know and I'm sorry for going off but I've been so stressed out lately." "Going out will do you some good; hopefully we'll hook up with some ballers tonight."

Chapter Seven

When Tasha and Roxanne arrived at the club the line was wrapped around Ocean Drive. "It's no way we're getting in," Tasha said. "You stay here and I'll see whose working the door tonight," Roxanne replied. Roxanne prayed that she ran into one of her people because this was one show she refused to miss. "Ma'am you need to step back," an arrogant security guard spoke. "I'm looking for David, has he arrived yet?" "I don't know any David and I'm not going to say it again; step back!" "Do they pay you to be this rude?"

Roxanne pulled out her cell phone and called David; he was their only hope. He didn't answer his cell so she called him at home. David use to be a small time drug dealer from Haiti that had promoted to king pin status in a matter of months. He knew the Feds were watching him and it was only a matter of time before they ran up and auctioned everything he risked his life for. Instead of doing Fed time or turning state's property he decided to get out the game and invest his money into all the major concerts that came through Miami and Haiti. "Jones residence," a Haitian woman answered. "Greetings, is David in." "May I ask whose speaking?"

"Roxanne." The lady put Roxanne on hold and called out to David to pick up the phone. "Roxy, what's up lil mama? We rode by your house today to see if you wanted to roll with us tonight." "What's happening tonight," Roxanne asked. "We had back stage passes to see LL." "That's why I'm calling you. Me and Tasha are here in this long line waiting to get in.

I asked this rude ass security guard at the door if he knew you but, he started acting like he was the star and everybody is here to see him." "I should be there in ten minutes so why don't ya'll just wait for me and we can go in together." "That'll work, so I'll see you in ten," Roxanne said in relief.

Roxanne walked back to tell Tasha the good news. She was in the same spot that Roxanne left her in. "Any luck." "I just talked to David and he's going to get us in." "You know David likes to come when the show is almost over," Tasha said. "No, he promised he would be here in ten minutes. Let's start walking to the front." David arrived twenty minutes later and about ten deep. "What happened to ten minutes," Roxanne asked. "You know a nigga had to get right," David replied. "Whatever, all that matters is that you're here; now let's party," Roxanne said.

Tasha and Roxanne collected their passes and headed straight to the bar. "Don't go too far, I wanna introduce ya'll to LL," David yelled. Tasha almost fainted; meeting LL was something that she only dreamed about. Tasha wished Sean could see her now, hanging out with the heavyweights in V.I.P. Her wishes became a reality when she bumped into Tommy.

"Tasha, I didn't know you were gonna be here tonight," Tommy said surprised to see her. "Yeah, I didn't know you were gonna be here either. Is Sean here with you?" "No, he's in L.A.," Tommy responded. Everything that Tasha did or planned to do she did it to the tenth power because she knew Tommy would be watching her every move to report it back to Sean. The only thing she didn't plan on was seeing Andre. She quickly turned her back away from the crowd praying that he hadn't seen her. She pulled

Roxanne down on the sofa with her and pretended to be in deep conversation. "What's going on girl," Roxanne asked.
"Dre just walked in."

"What's the problem; Sean's not here." "I know but, Tommy is," Tasha said in a panic. "Oh shit, you better go down there and handle your business before that fool embarrasses all of us." "What if Tommy sees me with him." "Don't worry about Tommy I'll distract him."

Roxanne walked over to Tommy with a bottle of Moet. "Have a drink with me," Roxanne asked. "What's the occasion," Tommy asked. "No occasion, we just need to talk." "What could we possibly have to talk about?" "I know you and Sean are like brothers and you know Tasha and I are like sisters. I honestly think she needs to move on but she's like stuck on stupid when it comes to him. I really need to know what his intentions are because I'm so tired of seeing her cry all day over someone that could care less," Roxanne said.

"As far as I know there are no intentions. They had a fling that resulted in what she says are his babies but we all know who he always runs back to. Tasha's a cool girl and I hate to see her messed up like that but that was pretty messed up how she did her own cousin. You know niggas will try you just to see how far they can go and she obviously failed the test," Tommy exploded. Tommy and Roxanne were so deep into conversation that Roxanne hadn't notice the commotion going on downstairs.

"Who you here with," Dre asked Tasha. "Roxanne. I didn't know you were coming," Tasha responded. "Who's watching my kids?" "Dre I already told you Sean is all over that." "Forget that wanna be playa, everybody but that fool knows those kids belong to me." "I'm not doing this tonight. I'm going to find Roxanne." "You're done here we're going home."

Dre grabbed her arm and pulled her across the dance floor. Tasha was so upset that Dre would even handle her like this and before she knew it, she had slapped him so hard that his two-carat diamond earring flew out of his ear. "Let go of me I'm not leaving with you," Tasha cried out. "You don't think I saw you upstairs trying to hide from me. Maybe I need to go up there and have a conversation with Tommy since his boy is always missing in action." "Dre please don't do this. If that's what you want I'll leave with you," Tasha pleaded. "I thought you'd see it my way."

Tasha was walking so fast to reach the exit door that she didn't have a chance to tell Roxanne she was leaving. Tasha was more disappointed than anything because Dre had ruined her night and her once in a lifetime chance to meet LL Cool J. Tasha walked behind Dre with tears falling from her eyes. Dre opened Tasha's door to his 1964 Classic Impala and kissed her on the cheek. Tasha pulled away. "This is best for all of us; you'll see," Dre said.

The ride was long and tense from South Beach to Ft. Lauderdale "I know you hate me right now but, I have every right to know if those kids are mine. Instead of looking for a quick come up you need to focus on what's more important; those kids having their real father in their life. Of course I don't have the money Sean has and I can't fly you all around the world and lace you in diamonds but we have history and I've loved you since I was twelve." "I can't just walk away I'm in too deep.

I've already hurt too many people," Tasha exposed. "You have nothing to be ashamed of. Every woman wants to be rescued from the hood and you saw your chance and took it. I can't hate on that I can only respect it." Tasha sobbed uncontrollably. She cried for Sean, Dre, her kids and me. She thought back to the day when I had caught her in bed with Sean and the look on my face. She thought about Sean who had moved her out of Liberty City into a nice three-bedroom apartment down south. And when she told him she was pregnant he never once said, "Why are you calling me, it's not mine" or "Here's the money for an abortion."

She thought about Dre; how she, Monica and I had met him at Bayfront Park when we were still running around in ponytails and training bras. She thought about the kids; how instead of being a nurturing mother she spent every waking moment plotting on how she was going to steal Sean away from me; her cousin.

"What have I done? How could you have the least bit of interest in me," Tasha sobbed. "I breathe you and that will never change. Remember when the ice cream truck came thru our hood and we were always the first ones there so we could eat our ice cream cones on the swings together." Tasha managed to crack a smile. "Those were the days. How do we get those back," Tasha asked. "They have always been here waiting for you to remember them," Dre responded.

They arrived at Dre's house at about twelve midnight. He had a nice four-bedroom house in Ft. Lauderdale that he'd bought before the accident. Dre was the all around athlete in high school. He played baseball, basketball and football. He had every school in the country scouting him but he decided to pass on college and play football with The Miami Dolphins.

Life was great for him and Tasha; he was voted Rookie of the Year and Tasha was expecting their first child. The last game of the second season he was tackled from behind and his neck was broken. Doctors presumed he would never walk again and his career was over. It seemed as if that was the only news worth reporting because every time you turned a channel or picked up the newspapers there were reports of Andre's accident.

Tasha became so stressed out with the interviews and taking care of Dre hand and foot that she ended up losing the baby.

That hurt Dre more than the end of his career. Tasha saw to it that Dre made a full recovery, but she ended up resenting him for the lost of her baby. The football money only stretched so far with all the hospital, doctor, mental and physical therapy bills. He started taking classes at The Miami-Dade Community College for Business Management.

When he received his degree he still couldn't find a job that would pay him the money he was use to. He started a non-profit organization with Miami Parks and Recreation that talked to young men about the positives and negatives of going pro before you've earned a degree to fall back on. He begged Tasha to join him in the cause but she had other plans on her agenda. Dre had become so involved in his work that he hadn't touched her in months.

She begun going out every night hooking up with any guy that showed her the slightest interest. Gossip started to get back to Dre about how promiscuous Tasha had become that when she returned home one morning, all of her things were on the front porch and the locks had been changed. Tasha begged to come back but Dre decided to let her go and experience the world since he was the only relationship she had since she was eleven.

He figured she needed to spread her wings and come back home when she'd had enough of flying. Two years passed without them speaking and it wasn't until the funeral that they bumped into each other. Tasha vowed that she had everything out of her system and was ready to be back into a committed relationship.

Dre never changed a word or asked a million questions he drove her to get her things and she went back home as if nothing ever happened. Tasha opened the door with her keys and headed straight for the shower. "Will you join me," she asked Dre. He jumped in the shower and begin washing her long silky hair and massaging her back. Her tears mixed in with the running water as she thought about how romantic he was and why she longed for another man's affection when she already had it with him.

"What's wrong," Dre asked. "I had a long day and I'm just tired." He carried her out of the shower, dried her off and lotion her from head to toe. This turned her on more than anything. She kissed him on his lips and he kissed her back with a passion that only true lovers know. She lay back on the bed waiting for him to have his way with her. "Make love to me," she whispered over and over. "There's plenty of time for that. Tonight I just want you to lay your head on my chest and leave all your worries and fears on my shoulders."

They were so close that the rhythm of their heartbeats became one. Tasha reminisced about losing her virginity to him when she was thirteen and how neither one of them knew what they were doing. She even recaptured the moment she announced to him she was pregnant and how he had given a box of Cuban Cigars to each one of his boys. She remembered delivering a still born baby boy and how he kicked so hard inside of her that everybody swore he was destined to be a football star just like his daddy.

She couldn't fight the tears anymore and burst out with a cry as if she were a soldier's wife and just got the news that her husband would never return home. "What happened? Tell me what's wrong."

"I miss him Dre." "Miss who?" "Our son, I want my little boy back. Why did God do this to us? What did I do that was so bad that he had to punish me this way? He could have taken me." "We shouldn't question God because he never makes a mistake. Everything happens for a reason. It took me a long time to come to that conclusion. I miss him too but we have to focus on the children that are here." Dre rocked her so gently that she cried herself to sleep.

He slipped away to call Tasha's mom. "Ha mom, it's me Andre." "Is everything alright baby?" "Oh yes ma'am everything's fine. I was wondering if you could keep the kids for a few more days I wanted to do something special for Tasha. She had a really hard time tonight. I had no idea she was still taking the miscarriage so hard." "When a woman loses a baby a part of her dies with it and you never really become yourself again." "I just didn't know it was this bad. She cried herself to sleep you know."

"I know baby, I think it's a combination of this situation with Sean and Angel as well. You take all the time you need and don't worry about the kids; they are in good hands. I'm glad you two are working it out because there are no two people that deserve to be happy more than you and Tasha." "Thanks mom." Dre sat up all night watching Tasha sleep. He wanted to make sure if she woke up with any nightmares he would be right there to console her. She woke up at seven to get ready for her appointment at the beauty school.

While she showered, Dre prepared ham and cheese omelets and fresh orange juice for them to enjoy on the screened porch. "All of this for me? You're too good to me." "So are you excited about touring the school this morning?" "I can't wait; you know how long I've wanted this. I have to become something that my kids can be proud of." "Why don't you drive the Excursion and when you're done come back here because I have something special planned for us." "My mother is bringing the kids back today." "I already handled that; I talked to her last night and she's going to keep them for a few more days."

"So tell me what you have planned?" "It's a surprise. You'll see when you return." Tasha kissed Dre goodbye. Dre quickly cleared the dishes from breakfast and was out the door. He had tons of shopping to do if he was going to make this night unforgettable. He bought five dozen red and white roses from the Cubans on the corner. He loaded up on lobsters, shrimp, chocolate, wine, strawberries, grapes, whipped cream and white candles. He had it all planned out. First a limo would take them to The Brian McKnight Concert and while they were there his sisters would come set up.

Tasha arrived fifteen minutes early and headed straight for the receptionist's desk. "I have a nine o'clock appointment with Mrs. Anderson." "And your name ma'am?" "Natasha Presley." "Have a seat and she will be with you in a moment. I'm sorry I almost forgot a package arrived for you this morning." Tasha took the package and opened it. Sean did exactly as he promised. There was a certified check for twelve thousand dollars made out to The Miami Beauty School. A slim model type woman walked up to her.

"You must be Natasha," Mrs. Anderson spoke. "Yes and I presume you're Mrs. Anderson." "Yes darling and welcome to The Miami Beauty School. May I offer you some coffee or tea?" "No thank you I'm fine," Tasha declined. "First I'll take you on the floor then we will tour the classrooms and let you meet the instructors." "Sounds good." "Once you've passed the appropriate tests you will be allowed on the floor to do actual client's hair to earn your graduating credits."

Mrs. Anderson took her to the classrooms where classes were already in session. What most of the students were doing or trying to do she already knew how to do it. "This is where most of our students drop out at. They can't handle the pressure of all the testing that's done to ensure you're ready. We don't tolerate mediocre work here because our prestigious reputation is on the line. If you decide to attend this school when you leave here you will be able to style the queen's hair," Mrs. Anderson boasted. "That's exactly the type of school I'm looking for." "Fabulous darling; come into my office."

Mrs. Anderson's office looked like it was taken from a page out of a magazine. There were awards and trophies everywhere. "You have a very nice office here," Tasha complimented her. "Decorating is one of my secret passions." "So, the next class starts in about three weeks." "Yes, that's right. Just to let you know we offer payment plans if financial aid is not obtainable." "That won't be necessary I would like to pay my entire tuition upfront." "That's even better. Let me get you to fill out some paperwork and get you registered for August and you will be all set. Do you have any questions for me?"

"Is there anything I need to bring with me on the first day?" "Everything will be provided for you and you will also receive your kit on that day as well." "I'm so excited; I don't think I can wait until August." "We are excited to have you as apart of our family and I demand exceptional things from you." "I won't let you down." "I'm going to hold you to that. These are copies of your paperwork and your receipt and I look forward to seeing you in class on August thirteenth."

Tasha left feeling that she had finally accomplished something. She called Sean. "Sean what's up; it's Tasha." "What's going on?" "I received the check this morning and I start classes on the thirteenth of next month."

"Good; I'm happy for you if that's what you want." "You already know what I really want." "So how was LL last night," Sean asked. "How would I know that?" "Wasn't you there?" "Maybe, who's to say?" "I heard your girl was going crazy looking for you. Didn't you leave with Dre last night?" "And you know this because?" Tasha wondered how he found out about the events that took place at the club all the way from L.A. "Nothing happens in South Beach that I don't know about." "So what if I did leave with Dre; what do you care?" "I don't; just make sure those tests results come back the way you say." "And if they don't?" "You don't wanna know the answer to that question." "Why do we always have to have hostile conversations?" "Because you're a classless bitch," Sean snapped.

"I wasn't a bitch when you was hooking up with me. Don't blame me for you losing Angel; you did that all on your own. I didn't force you to do anything you didn't wanna do. You need to try and be nice to me because I'm all you got since Angel left you. I heard it was something like a month ago. Yeah you're not the only one that can get information," Tasha informed him. "What goes on between Angel and I is not your concern." "It is when you shit on everybody and continuous disrespect me."

"You're right I'm sorry. My mother didn't raise me to treat women this way and I wouldn't want any man to treat my daughters the way I've treated you. But I meant what I said, what we had is over." "You expect me to let you just walk out of my life like that." "How do you expect us to move forward and be parents when every time we talk you're always on the same bullshit." "I'm dealing with the choice you made to end our relationship but I don't understand why we can't be friends with benefits."

"You never stop; do you," Sean said laughing and hanging up at the same time. Tasha drove to Roxanne's house. She knew what awaited her behind the closed door but she rung the bell anyway. "Oh now you decide to show up. If you were not my best friend I would beat your ass all up and down this street. Do you know how worried I was last night," Roxanne went off. "I know; it wasn't my fault. I went downstairs to talk to Dre and he ended up dragging me out of the club."

"So none of the phones in Miami were working?" "They were but I was so emotional last night that it slipped my mind." "What the hell happened anyway?" "All I remember is going downstairs to get rid of Dre we exchanged words and him dragging me out of the club. You were so busy laughing it up with Tommy that you didn't even see me trying to signal for you." "I was trying to keep Tommy occupied." "Some good that did because Sean knew about everything." "Stop lying bitch." "I'm serious, I just hung up with him and he was like your girl was looking all over for you, after you left with Dre." "Get the hell outta here," Roxanne said in disbelief.

"I was just as surprised as you." "So was he upset?" "He said he wasn't but you know how men be trying to act like they don't give a damn when they do." "How are you going to juggle Sean and Dre when they both hate one another?" "I don't know; I'm just so confused." "If it were me I wouldn't waste my time or energy on either one of them. Both of them are controlling and too damn busy for even their own lives. One is in love with another woman that happens to be your first cousin and the other is in love with his job. I don't understand what you have to be confused about." "They also have things about them that drives a bitch insane." "You can buy a no drama dick at the store." "It's not the same. I need a man to hold me and whisper sweet nothings in my ear." "Even if it's a lie?" "Even if it's a lie," Tasha replied.

"Whatever; to each is own. What's up for tonight?" "I'm chilling with Dre tonight. He's planning this top secret surprise for me." "One good thing I can say about him is that he's always doing sweet things for you," Roxanne admitted. "He's always been that way and I should love him more than I do but you know how we are always attracted to the bad boys that never call when they say they will or show the least bit of interest in you even when they know you're the shit."

"When do you get your test results?" "In a few weeks." "Are you scared?" "I'm trying not to think about it. I'm not too worried about what Dre would do but Sean; I don't want to even dream about what that boy would do." "Well whatever happens you know I got your back; way back." "Some friend you are." "You know I'm just playing with you." "What time is it," asked Tasha. "It's almost seven o'clock." "Oh shit I have to go. I'll call you tomorrow."

Tasha rushed out the door and headed up 95 to Ft. Lauderdale. She thought about calling Dre to apologize for being late but he hadn't called to complain about where she was so she left it just as that. When she pulled into the driveway the house was completely dark.

"Good, I beat him home." Tasha opened the door with her keys and gasped for air at what she saw. The floor was covered with red and white rose petals and there were candles everywhere. Tasha noticed a note on the kitchen table that read:

My Queen,

Go to the guest bedroom and you will find a white dress with the matching shoes. I can just imagine how beautiful you're going to look. Hurry up though because the limo will pick you up at nine o'clock and bring you to me.

Love,
Andre

Tasha just stood there for a moment trying to imagine what could be more beautiful than this. She wondered why he had left the dress in the guest room and not their room. It was already eight thirty so she didn't have time to play detective. She took a quick shower and ran into the guest room to get dressed. The dress was more elegant than she pictured it would be.

The shoes and the accessories were all on point. 'I know he had help with this,' Tasha thought out loud. It was five after nine so she looked out the curtains for the limo. There was a black stretch limo parked on the side of the street. She grabbed her purse and rushed out the door. The limo driver was waiting by the door.

"Good evening Ms. Natasha," the driver spoke as he opened the door. When he opened the door the limo was filled with white roses and another note:

"Stop smiling this is only the beginning."

The anticipation was killing her so she knocked on the glass and asked the driver. "Excuse me sir; where are we headed?" "Sorry ma'am, I'm not at liberty to say." She sat back enjoyed the ride and smell of sweet roses. She couldn't wait to see Dre and put her arms around him. She thought about all the love making that he would be getting all night and morning for this. Twenty minutes into the ride they stopped at a little building that looked like a jazz club spot. Tasha was looking out of her window trying to figure out where she was that she hadn't noticed Dre opening the door on the other side.

"Ha beautiful," Dre said. "Oh baby this is so sweet." Tasha got out the limo and began kissing Dre until he pulled away. "Come on let's go inside I have something special for you to see." As Dre walked Tasha inside there he was in living color Brian McKnight singing "All at Once." Tears begin to flow down Tasha's face. "Baby, I can't believe you did this. I had no idea he was in town."

The event was so intimate that there was even a dance floor for all the couples. Dre escorted her to the middle of the floor. She laid her head on his shoulder, closed her eyes and escaped into another world. His hands moved from her back to her butt and under her dress. He touched her so softly that her nipples protruded through her dress. As his fingers went deeper she let out soft moans. She grabbed his face kissing his forehead and then his lips.

"I could stay like this with you forever." "That's exactly what I was thinking." Dre reached in his pocket, got down on one knee and grabbed Tasha's hand. "Dre what are you doing?" "I love you more than I love myself. You're the first thing I think about when I wake up, you're the only woman I dream about when I'm sleeping and you're the last thing I think about when I fall asleep. Would you make me the luckiest man in the world and marry me?" "Are you serious?" "Yes, will you marry me?"

"Yes. Yes of course I'll marry you." "She said yes," Dre yelled into the crowd. Everybody looked back not knowing what was going on until they saw Dre still on one knee. They applauded and cheered for the newly engaged couple. Tasha hugged Dre and whispered in his ear. "Let's go home. I can't stand it anymore." They left the club with everyone still clapping as they walked out. As soon as they got in the limo it was on. They couldn't keep their hands off of each other.

Kissing led to touching and touching led to Dre easing her panties off. They made love all over that limo, from the seats to the floor. They were so into it they haven't heard the driver announce they were home. To be courteous he knocked on the door before opening it. "I think we've stopped," Tasha said. Tasha pulled down her dress, Dre zipped up his pants and he carried her inside to finish what they started. They headed straight to the bedroom.

When Dre opened the door, rose petals were all over the bed and white candles were placed all around the bed. Beside the bed lay a bowl of strawberries, chocolate and whipped cream. "When did you have time to do all of this? This is like something from a movie. A girl could get use to this." "Do you trust me?" "Yeah why," Tasha said in hesitation. Dre took a scarf blindfolded her and tied her hands to the bedposts. He teased her with strawberries before feeding them to her. Then he went on to pouring chocolate all over her body and licking every smudge away.

When he spread whip cream in between her legs she went crazy as his tongue went on an expedition. He took the blindfolds off and untied her leaving her wanting more. "Don't stop," Tasha screamed. "Believe me I'm not even half way done. Come shower with me; I fixed dinner for you." "I can't eat at a time like this. My body is on fire don't leave me like this." He flipped her over and took her from behind until she couldn't take anymore.

"I've never seen this side of you before. What movies you been watching?" "You know me better than that. What's in you is going to come out. No movie or book can teach you how to make a woman feel good; it can only expand on what you already know. You ready to eat now." "Yes! I need to get my energy up if I'm going to keep up with you," Tasha admitted.

They showered and ate steamed lobsters, potatoes and vegetable medley. They fed each other key lime pie for dessert. Drippings of pie filling fell between her breasts. Dre licked it off as if this was an invitation to start things up again. "There you go starting trouble again." She took the rest of her pie and rubbed it in his face. He grabbed the whole pie and throw it at her; getting it all over her face and hair. She picked up the whipping cream can and started spraying him everywhere. She chased him all over the house and down the hall where he was hiding behind the bedroom door. Soon as he saw her back he jumped out.

"You asshole you scared the shit out of me." They both laughed. They went back up front to see what damage they had done to the place. Pie and whipped cream was all on the walls and floors. "This place is a mess," Dre said. "You have to admit that was a lot of fun and that's all that really matters." "As long as we keep fun and excitement in our relationship we'll stay married forever."

"I just can't believe I'm an engaged woman now. You're not going to wake me up in the morning and tell me this has all been a dream; are you?" He picked her up threw everything off the counter and made love to her right in the kitchen. They moved from the kitchen to the floor from the floor to the shower and to the shower back into the bedroom. This went on up into the morning. They were exhausted and slept the day away.

Dre finally awoke that evening and kissed Tasha good-bye. "Where are you going?" "To The Jamaican Store; you want something back?" "A small curry chicken with a guava juice." She wanted to get up but her entire body ached. She took some Motrin and rolled back over to sleep for a few more hours. Her cell phone was ringing with back-to-back calls. She was still basking in the glow of last night and did not want any drama or bad news messing up her mood. 'Something could be wrong with the kids or Dre,' she thought. She opened up one eye to see who was calling, Roxanne.

"What bitch," Tasha answered as if she were waking up from a hang over. "You and Dre still held up over there sexing each other crazy." "You know it." "I assume you're not going out with us tonight." "My legs hurt so bad I can't even walk. We went to bed at five this morning. I have so much to tell you but I'm too tired to go through it all. I can tell you he asked me to marry him at Brian McKnight's Concert." "I didn't know he was here." "We're slipping because we always know whose coming to Miami."

"What did you say?" "I said yes." "I hope you know what you're doing. What about Sean?" "Of course I still love him, but I know I'll be happy and safe with Dre. I don't have to compete or beg for Dre's love. Besides, Sean says he's done with me." "What if he wants to start things up again? Then what would you do?" "I don't have an answer for that." "Then you're not ready to marry Dre. Do whatever you have to do to get him out of your system before you say I do. That's when the price of cheating costs."

"The only time I've ever cheated on Dre is when he started that damn foundation and he forgot I existed. I would never cheat on him under normal circumstances. We've been through the worst and best of times together and he knows me inside and out. He knows my moods just by the tone of my voice and he knows what I'm thinking even before I say it. I guess you could say we're soul mates no matter how hard I've been trying to fight it." "I'm not the one who needs convincing. When do you plan to break the news to Sean?"

"I should call him right now just to rub it in his face. Since Angel left him he's getting more arrogant by the day. It's damn near impossible to have a decent conversation with him."

"Baby I'm back," Dre yelled as he entered the house from the garage. "I'm in the room," Tasha yelled back. "You still in the bed?" "I can't get up my legs hurt." "Do you want your food in here?" "Please." "Who's that," Roxanne asked. "It's just Dre he went to get Jamaican Food." "Tell him I said what's up." "Roxanne said what's up." "Tell her I said what's up."

"I'll call you later I'm going to eat with my man." Tasha hung up the phone and ate dinner with Dre while watching "What's Love Got to Do with it." "If you ever hit me like that I will kill you, married or not. That's just not natural for a man to continuously beat the hell out of a woman for no reason. I never understood the domestic violence thing.

Why would you want your man or woman walking around all black and blue? You're making love to your woman but her eyes are all closed up and blood shot. Her face is distorted and unrecognizable. That's not attractive at all." "What man lets a woman beat up on him," Dre asked.

"It's a lot of men that are being abused by their wives or girlfriends. You just don't hear about it as much because they're probably embarrassed as hell." "They should just leave." "It's easier said than done. My friend went through that for five years with her baby's daddy; who just so happens to be a famous rapper. He would kick her ass for no apparent reason. If the label complained about his album sales or if radio neglected to put his song in rotation he would fight her like she was a man.

He chased her out the house naked many nights and dared her to take their son. We would always tell her to leave and she would leave for a day or two but, he would start crying, begging and saying how he wasn't going to do it anymore."

"Did he change?" "Hell no, it seemed like he beat her worse. It's not like she couldn't get anyone else. When I tell you this bitch was bad; Cuban and Black with long jet-black hair, skin like it was airbrushed and intellect beyond her years. When she got with this fool you would have thought she was a crack head. She stopped doing her hair; she would walk around in anything. You know how crazy me and Roxanne are."

"Crazy's not the word." "Whatever. We would be wild'n out and she wouldn't even laugh; she would sit there the whole time with her head down." "What's there to laugh about when a niggas going upside your head every night? You almost got it in the club the other night."

"Boy you know better." "You're right I do; I would never lay a hand on you. Let's go to the Key West tomorrow," Dre suggested. "That sounds like fun. It's sad that we're so close to Key West and we've never been there." "You'll love it." "How do you know? Who have you been there with?" "That's not important." "Stop playing. Don't make me hurt you."

Dre pulled her closer to him and they snuggled for the rest of the night. They woke up early the next morning excited what Key West had in store for them. "How long should I pack for?"

"Just a few days; if we don't have enough we will buy what we need when we get there." The bridge seemed to go on for days. Tasha was scared to be driving so high above the water.

"How long is this bridge anyway?" "It's about thirty miles long. If you don't like bridges or water, Key West is definitely not the place for you." "I see that now. Look that sign says Cuba is only ninety miles away. We are just too close to everything not to see it all. I would really love to go to the Bahamas. I heard it's a thirty minute boat ride." "Let's plan to go next weekend with the kids." "They'll love that; they have never been out of Miami."

They checked in at The Key West Hotel mid afternoon. They spent enough time there to shower and change clothes. Dre went to The Tackle and Bait Shack to buy shrimp for their fishing trip. He put the bait on her fishing pole and threw it out. "How do I know if I'm getting a bite?" "When you see that red and white ball go under but you have to pull it in quickly before it gets away."

Once Tasha got the hang of it she was catching fish after fish. They would catch one fish only to throw it back to catch the next one. They sat on the docks with their shoes off talking into the evening. "You know, no one has ever taken me fishing before. This was so peaceful; we have to do this more often," she said. "I plan to do a lot of things for you that no one has ever done.

You don't have to have all the money in the world to make moments unforgettable. It's like when we were kids and our parents bought us all that expensive stuff for Christmas; only for us to end up playing with the smallest and cheapest thing." After the sun went down they packed up and headed to the restaurant for dinner. They chose Café West since it was close to the hotel and in walking distance. Tasha had no idea what to do so she let Dre plan all of their activities.

He signed them up for scuba diving, snorkeling and massages. "Who do you know in the hood that goes scuba diving or snorkeling? What the hell is snorkeling anyway?" "We have to broaden our horizons no matter where we're from. Just because you're from the hood doesn't mean you have to live in that box."

"You still didn't answer my question; what is snorkeling?" "When you snorkel you wear this mask while swimming above the water to watch marine life on the bottom of the ocean." "You got me doing some crazy stuff. You do know I'm gonna loose credibility for this one." "We can always do something else."

She didn't want to sound ungrateful so she agreed to go along. She saw things she had never seen before, yet along knew existed. She noticed things about the water that she hadn't noticed before, the taste, the smell and how it seemed to never end. When all of their adventures were over they headed straight for the clubs. They hit up every club in Key West and partied up until the day they left.

Chapter Eight

"Tommy my flight lands at four. I need you to pick me up from the airport," is the message Sean left on Tommy's voice mail. When Tommy checked the message it was already three fifteen. He threw on some sweats and ran out the door. When he arrived at Miami International the traffic was crazy. Taxis, Shuttle Buses and Limos were blocking every possible view of Sean coming out of Baggage Claim.

He thought about parking the truck and going inside to wait for him but he wanted it to be a quick run to the truck pick up. Whenever Sean came through the airport it was always some kind of fan frenzy. He never had problems with signing autographs or taking pictures. It was his crew that had to deal with screaming girls fainting and digging their nails into their arms, trying to get to him or out of disbelief that he actually spoke to them and the guys that wanted to get in the music game that talked his ears off, about how hot their music was and how they were just trying to get on.

Then the worst was when they had to deal with those niggas that came like the devil; to steal, kill and destroy. It was going on four so Tommy hoped that Sean had turned his phone back on.

"Yo son where you at," Tommy asked when he got Sean on the phone. "I'm getting off the plane now." "Come down to the Delta Terminal. I'm in the White Escalade. Don't be stopping for no autographs, police are bugging out here." Sean put on his Versace Sunglasses and walked straight through the terminal. Tommy was standing by the door waiving him over. Sean jumped in the car and they drove to Miami Beach.

"How was L.A.? Did we get the deal with the network?" "What's my name son? Hell yeah we got it; the money we asked for and we got all creative control." "You was there long enough; I thought I was gonna have to come get you." "Any word on Angel," Sean asked with hope in his face. "No. I have the best P.I. on the job and he still can't find her. It's like she disappeared without a clue. When she wants to be found you'll find her; she's just hurt right now. Her family's stinking rich and they have a lot of resources; she could be damn near anywhere."

"Son I lost my girl of eight years over a hood rat." They pulled up in Sean's circular driveway. "Check the mailbox for me. I haven't checked it in weeks; Angel always did that." He headed upstairs to his bedroom leaving Tommy outside. He couldn't wait to lay in his own bed and not a bed in some hotel that only God knows who slept in and did what.

He lay there thinking about how I would be waiting there when he got home from a long trip. He thought about how many times he had made love to me and how this was the very bed that our child was conceived on; the one he made me get rid of. Everything about this house was me; the color of the marble to the design of the indoor pool. He longed for me like a newborn longs for his mother's milk. My clothes in the closet still smelled of Gucci and Chanel Perfumes.

He went over to my bathroom and picked up my brush that still had strings of my long brown hair in it. He knew I wanted my space but he had to hear my voice. He picked up the phone and called me. "Hello." Sean held the phone before speaking trying to absorb anything of me he could. "Hello," I repeated again. "Angel Eyes it's me." "I know," I said keeping it short. "It's killing me that

I can't talk to you everyday and I don't know what's going on with you. I feel like I can't protect you anymore."

"Sean you really don't have to worry about me. Mentally I'm happier than I've been in a long time. I'm doing yoga two times a week and I live a stress and drama free life." "I closed the deal that we pitched to the network. We signed off on it yesterday so I'll be in L.A. most of the time now."

"I'm happy for you; that is exactly what we prayed for." "I want you to come with me." "That's not what I want anymore. I'm ready to settle down; get married and have a kid or two." "I want the same thing," Sean said hoping I would feel his sincerity and forget the life I was living without him. "I don't know how to tell you this but I wanted you to hear it from me." His heart was beating faster than it was on the day he found my last letter.

"I met someone and we've been dating for a while now. I'm not saying we're ready to make that step but, I can see myself being married to someone like him." The phone was completely silent. "Hello. Sean are you still there?" He was speechless for the first time. "Have you slept with him," Sean asked not knowing if he wanted to hear the answer. "Not that it's any of your business anymore but no I haven't slept with him."

Sean let out a sigh of relief. He didn't want to imagine another man touching what he use to have under lock and key. "Don't get me wrong, I want to share that experience with him. It's a part of me that still belongs to you and I haven't been able to let that go yet. The first time I danced with him it felt wrong because no man had ever been so close to me but you. He knows the kind of relationship I was in so he's been very understanding."

"Was our relationship that bad? It's not like I abused you or anything." "It wasn't abuse to the point where you put your hands on me but you cheated and had kids on me; that's not abuse? I remember when you would be on tour and I would call your room after I couldn't reach you on your cell and girls would be running around laughing in the background. I would sit in our big mansion and wonder who my man was sleeping with tonight. That's why the house in Miami Beach means nothing to me because I sat in that house alone many nights crying myself to sleep."

"I'm sorry for everything I put you through I would give my life if I could take it back. I was young and everything was new to me. I had to learn the hard way; if you're not grounded this industry will eat you up." "I know you're sorry but that doesn't erase what you've done or created. I want to forgive you and move on. Do you honestly think I want to start the whole dating process over again?"

"Then don't." "So I'm suppose to walk through life by myself; being lonely?" "Yes if it's not with me. Just make sure you don't let him touch you because it still belongs to me. Isn't that what you always told me?" "When we were together?"

"Sean you can't be serious of course; we're going to touch." "I'm getting sick just thinking about it. I'm not giving up on you. We are destined to be together." "Well if that's in God's plan then it will be. I have to go; I'm late for my yoga class."

"Can I call you tomorrow?" "You're only making it harder on yourself. What's the purpose of you calling me?" "As long as I can hear your voice my life is alright. I need a piece of you to hold on to while I'm in waiting."

"That's fine; tomorrow and tomorrow only." "That's good enough for me. I want you to know I haven't touched another woman since we made love that night. I love you baby." "I love you too."

He hung up with a smile not knowing if he should be happy that he wasn't completely written off. I could tell he was hurt that I had confided in him about my newfound love. He had to get me back before this man left his mark on me. He could only imagine what plans a man had to do with a woman's body this fine.

There was a knock on the bedroom door. "You dressed." "Yeah, come on in." "I checked the mail I think you want to see this one." It was a letter from A Paternity Testing Company. He held the letter in his hand and just stared at it. This letter determined the outcome of his life and whom he spent it with.

"You want me to open it," Tommy asked. "I got it; I just need to get my mind right. I've never been so nervous in my life. Sean slowly opened and unfolded the results.

The letter listed each child one by one:

In the case of Shawna Presley, Sean Crews is 99.9% excluded as the father.

In the case of Shanice Presley, Sean Crews is 99.9% excluded as the father.

In the case of Chanel Presley, Sean Crews is 99.9% excluded as the father.

In the case of Chantel Presley, Sean Crews is 99.9% excluded as the father.

He sat there with his face in his hands and his tears soaking up the paper. "What did it say?" He handed Tommy the letter. Tommy read it over and over again shaking his head.

"I knew she was scandalous. She knew she was sleeping around and she kept quiet about it." "Bring the Benz out; I'm going to deal with this bitch." "I can't let you do that. If you hurt or kill this girl your career is over."

"I don't give a damn. I gave her too many opportunities to tell me the truth. I took care of those kids for two, almost three years and I put that bitch into an apartment. Those kids call me daddy and you tell me I'm not the father. What am I suppose to do now? My girl's heart crumbled, when she found out that I had fathered kids with her cousin and made her get an abortion. It's probably that dude Andre kids. She's going to pay me back every dime that I spent on them kids or I'll take her lying ass to court. I want her and her kids out of that apartment tonight!"

"If you go promise me you won't hit her." "I can't promise you that; I'm so heated right now I wanna throw her off the building." "I'm going with you. Let's go."

"Tommy I have to do this by myself." "I wouldn't be your boy if I let you go over there in this state of mind. Come on I'll drive you."

Sean agreed but only if he was driving. He pushed that Benz to the limit trying to make it over there. He pulled up in front leaving the car on. "Sir you have to move your vehicle." Tommy turned the car off threw the keys to the valet and ran after Sean. He caught the elevator just before the door closed.

"Just don't do anything crazy," Tommy pleaded with him. They got off at the fifth floor and Sean headed straight for apartment five zero seven. He knocked and banged on the door. No one answered. "Maybe she got the results already and she's hiding out," Tommy suggested.

This infuriated him to the point that he began kicking the door with the sole of his Timberland Boot. He didn't stop until the door was completely kicked in. He searched every room, under the beds and in the closets looking for Tasha. She was nowhere to be found. They stayed there all night waiting for her to come home. "We need to go home. It's no telling when she'll be back." "I'm not leaving until I see her."

"It could be days." "Then I'll wait."

Tommy went to the back to call me; I was the only one that could talk sense into him. "Angel its Tommy I hate to call you so late but its Sean." "What happened? Is he hurt?" "Not yet. He got the results from the paternity tests and none of the kids were his." "What? Stop lying." "No really I'm serious. None of them and I know he's going to hurt this girl. He kicked in her door and we have been at her apartment all day waiting for her to come home. He's in a trance; he won't move he won't talk he's sitting there with his hand on his head staring into space. Please talk to him maybe you can at least get him to leave."

"Sure Tommy anything I can do." "It would be nice to see you two back together again. He's not the same since you left." "That's good; you're probably the only person that knows how wrong he did me." "He told me that you were seeing someone."

"I'm so happy with him; I never knew you could have a drama free relationship." "Even though he's my brother all I ever wanted was for you to be happy." "I know that's why I love you more than you will ever know." Tommy walked back up front and handed Sean the phone. "I'm not taking any calls," Sean said holding his hand in the air. "It's Angel," Tommy announced.

"Baby what's going on?" "They're not mine. The kids aren't mine. I swear I'm going to kill her," was all he murmured. "Baby please don't do anything to jeopardize your career; more so than that, your freedom. You're a man you can't put your hands on a woman they have laws against that. I know you're hurting in the worst way but please go home." "I need you to save me from myself. Please come home."

"If you promise me that you'll leave with Tommy right now and if you see Tasha you won't beat the shit out of her I'll fly in tomorrow." "If that's what you want." "That's what I want. Let me talk back to Tommy please." "He told me he was going to leave with you. I will be there tomorrow." "We're walking out right now. Do you need me to pick you up?" "No I'll take a taxi." I went upstairs to tell Monica what was going on.

I jumped in the bed and lay next to her. "You will not believe the news I just received live and direct from Miami." "Whatever it is, it has to be good coming in this late." "Sean got the results back today. He's not the father of any of the children. He went ballistic. Tommy had to call me just to calm him down. I told him if he left her apartment and went home I would fly in tomorrow."

"He needs to beat that ass. That bitch knew those babies weren't his. How long are you staying?" "A few days; long enough to get him back on track." "What do you think Gene will say?" "I think he'll understand. I gave him the whole run down of our relationship. He says he just wants me to be happy whether it's with him or Sean." "When Sean sees how tanned you are and your hair flowing all down your back he's going to try and rip your clothes off."

"I know, but I'm not going there for that. I hope I made that clear to him. Are you going to be alright here by yourself because you can always come with me?" "It's nothing for me in Miami right now."

I fell asleep in Monica's room and got up early the next morning and headed for the airport. I hadn't told them what time I was coming in for my own reasons. I still wanted to keep my location private.

Chapter Nine

I caught the first taxi I saw to Miami Beach. When I arrived at his house nothing had changed except for the new Bentley parked in the driveway. I unlocked the door and went down to the gym; where I knew he would be working out. When I walked in his workout was over and he was already hitting the showers. I sat on the weight bench waiting for him to come out. He came out wrapped in only a towel.

He had gotten finer. His six-pack was more defined and his arms were like a Michael Angelo Sculpture. He didn't speak when he saw me. He picked me up and carried me upstairs. We kissed and hugged until he took my hand and led me to the kitchen.

"It looks like you have been taking real good care of yourself. This is like a dream to have you standing here. I can't believe you're really here." "I would never let you destroy yourself. You're not looking to bad yourself," I said rubbing his chest. He lifted up my shirt to look at my stomach. "You want to tell me why you did that." "I wanted to see how big my baby was getting." "There's not a baby." "Is that what the doctor said?"

"No. I haven't seen a doctor." "When was your last period?" "I can't remember." "I'm taking you to the doctor in the morning." "That's not why I came, besides I only have a few days before I go back home." "You are home and I hope you know I'm not letting you leave." "Whatever. What's for breakfast?" "We can go to South Beach for breakfast." "Why don't we stay in and you cook for me. I have really missed your French toast. While you cook you can tell me what happened." "Go upstairs and look on the night stand the letter is under my wallet."

I walked upstairs and picked the letter up. I looked around and everything was exactly how I left it. It wasn't a single garment or shoe out of place. All of my perfumes were still separated by designer. When I made it downstairs; he was just finishing up our breakfast. We set up everything on the island of the kitchen. "Thank you baby this smells good."

"Where's the letter? Open it." As I started reading the results I was overcome with relief and anger. Why would a woman sleep around with several men at the same time without protection and get pregnant and not inform all of her sexual partners, but pen it on the man with the most money. I wasn't the one to hate on the hustle but when kids were involved it was a totally different game.

"I can't believe she would just carry this lie around all this time. Maybe she really didn't know." "That bitch knew. I asked her if it was any possibility that anyone else could be the father. She looked me dead in my eyes and told me it was no way. It would have been easier if she had of step to me with the truth. All she had to say was 'Sean you wasn't the only dude I was sleeping with and it's a chance you may not be the father.' She chose not to; that's why I gotta snatch her ass up."

"Have you tried to call her?" "There's nothing we have to talk about anymore." "You promised you wouldn't touch her. If you won't call her I will. Go get the phone please." "If you wanna talk to her; you get the phone. I don't want her number to be dialed on my phone or in this house period! That's how much I'm hating on her right now." "I'm here to help you but if you want to be a rude ass I'll go back home and you'll be on your own." He came from behind wrapped his arms around my neck and kissed me on my cheek. "I'm sorry."

I walked outside to call Tasha and Sean followed. She answered on the first ring. "What's up baby?" "It's Angel." "Oh Angel I'm sorry I thought you were Sean." "When I see you bitch it's on; 99.9% not my kids," Sean said yelling from the background. "Shhh," I said trying to shut him up while giving him an evil stare. He closed his mouth and walked back in the house.

"Angel, what's going on over there," Tasha asked. "It's just Sean and his friends playing around. Can you meet me for lunch? We need to talk." "Sure. Where should I meet you? I think this talk is long overdue." "Meet me at The Palm's in Coral Gables. I'll be in the back."

From her conversation I could tell she knew nothing about the paternity results. I went back inside to take a bath and dress for my lunch with her. I made sure to lock the bathroom door so I wouldn't be interrupted. I put on my yellow and white Versace dress and dabbed Versace perfume on my wrist and neck. I called Sean on the intercom to see where his location was.

He was in the office on a conference call with the label. I whispered that I was leaving. He motioned for me to come in and he put the call on hold. "This call just saved you." "From what?" "From me tearing that dress off of you. Where you going?" "I'm going to see my aunt. I won't be long." "Hurry back because I got plans for all of that." He kissed me good-bye and continued his call.

I took the keys to the Convertible Benz and headed to Coconut Grove. I arrived ten minutes early because I wanted to see her walk in. I sat there wondering how we came from the same bloodline and was so morally different. I ordered a pina colada for myself and if memory served me right; an amaretto sour for Tasha.

She arrived on time and hesitated to hug me not knowing if it was the right thing to do. "When did you get back?" "This morning." "Are you here to stay?" "I'm not sure," not wanting to give her too much information. "That dress looks nice on you. Who's it by?" "Versace; let's cut the small talk and get to the real reason I invited you here."

"Angel I'm sorry about what happened between Sean and me. I never meant for you to find out that way. I know we're family and I should have never crossed that line but you yourself know how easy it is to fall in love with him. I was so in love with him that I didn't care who I hurt."

"You had Andre. Did you stop and think that the truth would eventually come out. There are a million other men you could have slept with, why did you have to sleep with mine?" "I don't have an answer for that," Tasha said holding her head down. "I knew you wouldn't." "I just want us to get pass this and be friends again." "We will always be cousins because we were born into it but friends we will never be. If you're finished I would like to get to the real reason we're here."

I pulled out the letter from my Versace Bag and handed it to Tasha. "What's this?" I didn't say a word. My blood boiled inside just thinking about how she flaunted her kids in my face. She opened the letter and read it aloud. Her hands and body began to shake. "No. No. No. Oh my God; this can't be true," she screamed. "Where did you get this?" "Sean received it in the mail yesterday. He was ready and still wants to kill you. I had to fly here just so he wouldn't kick your ass. Why didn't you tell him you were sleeping with someone else?

You lied to this man and your kids for two and a half years about who their father was. You even got them calling him daddy. He's been taking care of the kids and probably you too and you didn't think he deserved the truth. I want you to know you made a fool out of the wrong man. You have dug a hole that your ass can't get out of." "I swear I didn't know. The only other person I was with was Dre but the times I slept with Sean and the times I got pregnant matched up perfectly that's why I never said anything."

"Maybe you should have." "What I'm I going to do Angel? What do I say to the kids? It's no telling what he's going to do to me. You have to help me; you're my only hope." "He promised me that he would not touch you but you need to be a woman and face him. On the other hand Sean is his own man. There are just some things he does that I don't have control over and in that case it's whatever."

I paid the waiter for our drinks and left. Everything I could have done to hurt her like she hurt me was accomplished but it didn't stop me from wanting to protect her. As I stood outside waiting for valet I contemplated on going back inside wrapping my arms around her telling her it would be alright and that we would get through this together.

My heart wasn't ready to let go of the hurt. I drove off and went to check on my house since I was in the area. The house was spotless as usual not a spic of dust anywhere. I had Maria cleaning only once a week since I was no longer living there. The mail covered the desk in the office. I flipped through the mail and discarded everything except the bills and two letters from my parent's attorney.

In Love With A Rap Star

I put the letters in my bag to open when I got back to the Bahamas. I thought about changing into a pair of my Roberto Cavalli Jeans and Shirt but I didn't feel like explaining myself to Sean as to what I was doing that needed a change of clothes. I parked the Benz in my garage and took the Suburban. No matter what vehicle Sean bought for me I was completely in love with my truck. My dad had surprised me with it at my twenty-first birthday party. My parents asked for a whole year what I wanted to do.

They said turning twenty-one was a milestone and they wanted to throw me the biggest party that Miami had ever seen. I declined on the party and told them I would rather have a small dinner party on our yacht with them, a few of my friends and Sean. Before I knew it, I was walking into a party with a guest list of three hundred people. Every celebrity that you could think of was there. Designers flew clothes in all the way from Milan. Every newspaper and magazine publication was there, snapping pictures and doing interviews. Sean wrote a song for me and performed it. The night just couldn't get any better.

In the middle of the party in drives this big black truck and the first man that I loved steps out; my dad handing me the keys to my new Suburban. Six months after that my parents died. I guess you could say that truck has sentimental value to me and Sean knew it that's why he never fussed at me for driving the cars he leased me for more than a couple of months.

I got in my truck and headed for Sean's house. I pulled up behind a black Rolls Royce, a red Porsche and a white Escalade. The truck looked like Tommy's but I couldn't be sure. "I hope I don't have guests to entertain," I said to myself. I got out the truck took my shoes off and the pins out of my hair letting it fall down my back and went through the back entrance. Sean was out back on the phone. I caught the tail end of the conversation but he was telling someone to get the girls together and that three e-tickets were waiting for them at the airport. When I walked pass him he grabbed my arm.

"Where you been all day?" "I had some business to handle. I'm exhausted babe I'm going to say good night." "Tommy's putting some steaks and lobsters on the grill." "I'm not that hungry you can send some fruit to the guest room. Tell Tommy I said good night and I'll talk to him in the morning."

"You brought company with you?" "No. I'm going to be staying in the guest room while I'm here." "How is that going to look? I know we're not together right now but don't treat me like every other man on the street. I need to feel you next to me. If you sleep in the guest room I'm sleeping in there with you."

Instead of causing a scene I agreed to sleep in the bedroom upstairs with him. I went upstairs to get ready for bed and he came soon after. He leaned against the sink and watched me shower. "I'm really trying to respect your wishes. Do you know how hard it is for me not being able to touch you?" "Hand me the towel please."

I pushed opened the shower glass and tried to squeeze past him since he wouldn't move. My body rubbed up against his and I could feel his erection. He closed his eyes and took a deep breath. I put on the biggest t-shirt I could find because everything I had there was lace or chiffon. "You're killing me here. You have to give me something to work with. If I can't touch you will you at least put on something sexy for me?"

"Would you just go back downstairs with your friends? Nobody told you to come up here to harass me anyway." "Your breasts have gotten bigger and you don't think it might be because let's see; you're pregnant." "Only bigger to you because you haven't seen me in a while. Would you go please?" "Yeah, I'll go but I'm not done with you yet."

Maybe he was right. My breast had gotten bigger and they were so sensitive that I couldn't stand water from the shower to hit them. Something in the back of my mind kept telling me to see a doctor. I didn't want it to be true and if it were he would never know. It was three in morning when he got into bed. I could tell he had been drinking he had the whole room smelling like Hennessey. I woke from the most wonderful dream to get a few things off my chest.

"I need to talk to you." "Right now; can't it wait till morning?" "I saw Tasha today. She had no idea what was going on until I showed her the papers. She was just as shocked as you. I'm not telling you not to be upset but give her the benefit of the doubt." "You really believe that. She told me it was nobody else. Did she at least tell you who the other person was?" "Andre." "I knew it and I bet he knew it too. I spent damn near half a million dollars taking care of her and Dre's kids. I just sent twelve thousand dollars to some beauty school she wanted to go to."

This was all news to me. I wondered what else he had kept from me. "You spent half a million dollars on her and I'm suppose to be happy about that. What could you have possibly spent that much money on in a two year period?" "It was all for the kids. I never bought her clothes, cars, jewelry or anything like that." "That still doesn't add up." "Angel just leave it alone." "There's something you're not telling me. How am I going to trust you again and your closets are overflowing with skeletons. I just want to hear from you what I already know." He looked at me like a scared little boy. "I don't wanna hurt you anymore." "There's nothing else that you can do to hurt me."

"When Tasha and I were messing around I bought a high rise apartment down south. Whenever we hooked up that's where it would happen. If I was in town she would call me and we would meet at the spot. I would do my thing break her off with some cash and be on my way. She was living back with her mom when she got pregnant and she didn't want to stay in Liberty City or move back with Dre so I moved her into the apartment.

I had every piece of furniture made and shipped direct from the factory to furnish that apartment. When the babies came they had more Gucci and Louis Vuitton than I did. I spent over fifty thousand in clothes alone. She never paid a bill or bought a crumb of food in that apartment. She was nothing like you."

"You thought she would be. Let me get this straight, you would go sleep with her, come home, be all over me and didn't use protection with me knowing that you had just went raw dog into another woman. That's nasty! What if you would have given me something? Then What?" "I didn't think about it that way." "Why even do it in the first place? I wasn't enough for you? I never deprived you of any sexual pleasures. I adored you and treated you like a king so you wouldn't have to look for it out on the road."

"I'm kicking myself trying to figure out what it was about her that made me step out of our relationship and I have not been able to come up with any explanation."

"Save it for someone else. I'm going to bed; I've heard enough." I rolled over closed my eyes and tried to go back to sleep. Sean rolled over behind me placing his hand on my stomach. I wanted to start a fuss about him touching me but I let him have his way instead. It felt good lying in bed and being touched by someone familiar.

I woke up the next morning to an empty house. The peace and quiet was just what I needed. I took a swim and went in the kitchen to duplicate Sean's French toast recipe. After I ate and cleared the dishes I went out back to absorb the sun.

Tommy and Sean were at the airport trying to find Sean's cousins that had just flew in from New York. He recognized them coming down the escalader and waited for them at the bottom. "How was the flight," Sean asked. "It was alright," Precious answered. "How's New York," Tommy asked Destiny. "New York is New York," she answered. They drove Sean's cousins around the corner to get a rental car. They made a request for tented windows. "Ya'll ready to do this," Sean asked. "Hell yeah where she at," they all said. "I'm taking you home first I don't want you linked to this," Tommy said. "I wouldn't miss this for nothing in the world. I won't feel better unless I see this with my own eyes."

A private investigator had been tailing Tasha every since the apartment drama. He had reported that she was at a house in little Haiti. Sean knew exactly where she was, Roxanne's house. Precious rang the doorbell, Destiny and Fatima hid on the side of the house. "Who is it," Roxanne asked. "Pizza delivery," she said holding a pizza box in her hand. Roxanne opened the door thinking

Tasha had ordered a pizza. When Precious heard the locks being unchained she motioned for her cousins.

As soon as Roxanne opened the door all three of them ran up on her locking her in the closet and dragging Tasha outside by her hair.

They kicked, punched and slapped her around like a rag doll. She tried to fight back but they were just too strong for her to take on. They kept her face down so she could not identify them. They didn't stop until she blacked out. "I think this bitch has learned her lesson," Fatima spoke after they had given Tasha a New York ass whipping. Sean and Tommy was down the block watching the whole thing.

When the fight was over they got in their rental car and flew back to New York. They left Tasha outside confused and bleeding. When she came to she managed to crawl in the house and call 911. She heard Roxanne banging and trying to kick the door open but she was too weak to open it. The police, ambulance and the fire trucks arrived. The paramedics ran to her aid. She pointed to the door where the noises were coming from.

The police approached the door with caution and weapons drawn but Tasha couldn't tell them that the person inside was a victim also. "Ma'am calm down it's the Miami PD; we're here to help you." They unblocked the door and let her out. Her eyes were blood shot red from crying. She ran over to Tasha and as she looked up Roxanne screamed.

"What have they done to you?" "Call Dre," Tasha said in a faint voice. "Ma'am, she's not able to speak right now so we need you to make a statement," an officer asked. "I can't give you much only that a girl knocked on the door and said she was delivering a pizza and when I opened the door they all grabbed me and locked me in the closet."

"How many were there?" "At least three or four. I don't know it all happened so fast. Is she gonna be alright?" "They seem to have her stable but you're welcome to ride in the ambulance." Roxanne called Dre and informed him about what happened and instructed him to meet them at Jackson Memorial.

When they arrived Dre was already there waiting in the Emergency Room. Tasha's face was so swollen; she couldn't open her eyes. Dre burst out crying and walked out the room. Roxanne walked behind him and tried to console him. "I know it looks bad but things could be worse. They could have killed both of us."

"Who did this? Did you get a good look at them?" "It happened so fast. If they passed me in the streets I wouldn't know it." "We have to call her mother." "I'll let you call; I can't be the one to bring her the bad news." Dre walked to the waiting room and called Tasha's mom. He prepared himself to be strong. "Praise the Lord," she said answering the phone. "Mom I have some bad news. Tasha's been hurt and you need to get to Jackson Memorial as soon as you can." The phone was silent. "Mom?" She didn't hang up or even say goodbye. He tried calling back but the line was busy. An hour later she was there.

Dre tried to prepare her for what she was about to see. They walked in Tasha's room hand and hand. When she saw her daughter's swollen face and bruised body she fell to the floor. "My baby, tell me who did this to you?" Roxanne brought the doctor in and introduced Ms. Presley as Natasha's mother. "What's going on with my baby? Why is she just lying there?"

"She was in a lot of pain on arrival so we have her heavily sedated. The swelling should go down in a few days but we just want to keep her here to run a few tests. There appears to be no visible bone fractures but we will still take her down for x-rays." They all stood there trying to put the pieces of the puzzles together.

Chapter Ten

Tommy dropped Sean off at the entrance gate and he walked the rest of the way. I was on the phone with Monica when he arrived. He came over to the sofa kissed my forehead and ran his hands through my hair.

"How was your day," he asked. "Quiet, how was yours?" "It was better than I could have hoped for."

He went off to do his thing and I continued my conversation with Monica. The way Monica and I were carrying on you would have thought we had been separated for more than two days. I promised to fill her in on every detail when I got home. I went from playing the piano in the music room to watching a movie in the theater room. I was bored out of my mind; this reminded me why I never stayed here.

It was only so much fun you could have in a house this big by yourself. I peeped in the office to see if Sean was in there; he was on another conference call. I went and sat in the chair in front of him. He waved for me to come over and sit on his lap. I sat down on his lap and we played spades with a deck of cards lying in the top drawer.

After beating him about five times I tried to get up and start packing for my trip home. He pulled me back down and tried to untie my bikini top. I popped his hand and rolled my eyes.

"How much longer," I whispered in ear. "We're wrapping up now," he whispered in mine.

I sat there for twenty minutes waiting for him to end his call. I got tired of waiting so I got up and walked out of the office. He immediately hung up the phone and ran after me.

"Where are you going?" "I'm going home. I came to be here for you but by the looks of things you seem to be handling everything just fine." "It only seems that way because you're here. What do you mean you're leaving?" "Don't start that with me; you knew I was only staying a few days. I left so fast I didn't have time to tell Gene I was leaving and he's probably worried out of his mind about me."

"Is that what all of this attitude is about. I could care less about this Gene guy.

You were mine first; eight years as a matter of fact." He walked up to me and put his hands in my bikini bottoms. "Does he touch you like this?" "You know he doesn't touch me like that. Our relationship is on a whole other level." "What friends? I know you inside and out. I know what makes you let out those little soft moans and those loud screams when I'm hitting it just right. You want to go home and leave all of this."

"Don't give yourself that much credit. You should know those things about me; you've had eight years to get it right. How would I know if you're even doing it right? You're the only guy that I've ever slept with."

"How many organisms do you have every time we have sex?" "Three; maybe four." "I rest my case." "Of course you would be the best in my eyes because I have no one else to compare you to."

I wasn't being completely honest with him because most of my girlfriends complained about their boyfriends or husbands sex life. Before they could even get into it yet alone have an organism their man was done and fast asleep. Sean was the total opposite. We never had sex less than an hour and he made sure I had not one, but multiple organisms. It had been months since I had any and I was about to explode.

I didn't want to admit it to him but I missed making love to him so when he invited me to take a bubble bath; I didn't think twice about my answer. He took my hand and led me upstairs. I waited in the bedroom while he got things ready in the bathroom. The mood had to be set just right if he was going to steal me away from this guy whom I had become involved with. 'If she's not pregnant now she will be before she leaves here,' Sean said to himself.

I knocked on the door thinking he had started without me.

"In a minute," he yelled through the door. He opened the door, standing there with nothing on. I wanted to skip the bath and get straight to the lovemaking. I walked in a bathroom surrounded by vanilla candles and the tub was filled with bubbles and rose petals. He helped me into the tub and got in behind me. He felt so good; I laid my head back on his chest as he gripped my breasts. We said nothing from our mouths instead letting our hands speak for us. All of his romantic gestures went to waste because we were out of the tub before our hands or feet had a chance to get wrinkled.

I got out and he followed me into the room. I pushed him down on the bed and opened the drawer where he usually kept all of his condoms. He took it out of my hand and threw it on the floor.

"We don't need that," he said, pulling me back down on top of him. "I don't want to get pregnant,"

I said not hinting to him that I thought I already was. I was so caught up in the heat of the moment I didn't even press the issue. I rode him like he was my favorite horse. Every move I made he screamed my name and begged me not to ever give my love to anyone else. He flipped himself on top of me and punished me for all the starvation I had taken him through over the months.

When we finished it was time for dinner. I heard about this new Italian restaurant in Coconut Grove so I made reservations for two. He dressed into a pair of Roberto Cavalli Jeans, shirt and blazer. I put on a red Armani dress with the matching Armani shoes. As soon as he saw me with his favorite dress on he ripped it off of me and backed me up against the wall.

"Sean what are you doing? We have to go. What about our reservations?" "You look so sexy in that dress; I can't help myself. Just give me ten minutes." "I'm not trying to shower again and not to mention you just tore up an eight hundred dollar dress." "I'll buy another one tomorrow."

"No! I want you to go downstairs and wait for me," I said standing there with half a dress on. I redressed in a Gucci Suit and hurried downstairs. Sean was waiting outside in a Mercedes Truck. "When did you get this?" "It's yours; they delivered it today." "It's not like I'm going to be here to drive it." "Why not," he asked with great seriousness in his eyes. "Let's just enjoy what we have right now."

He handed me the keys to my new car, let his seat back and closed his eyes.

"What are you thinking about?" "You," he responded. "What about me?" "I don't understand you. You just made love to me like I was the last man on earth; you say you still love me but you don't want to be with me. I can't live like this Angel."

"You of all people should know that just because you sleep with someone doesn't mean you're together. True; I love you and you're the only man I'm sexually attracted to but I've moved on and I'm not going back to all of your drama."

He just sat there not responding to anything else I had to say. We arrived at the restaurant and valet opened my door. Sean walked ahead of me leaving me outside. I often told him he had split personalities; one minute he could be the sweetest person and the next a complete jerk.

I walked in and he was already seated. I didn't want to be a bitch but I had enough of him acting like a spoiled little boy. I couldn't help but think I was the cause of it; catering to his every demand and need and never being able to say no to him. Enough was enough and I wasn't going to be his house groupie anymore. The waiter pulled out my chair for me.

"You look very nice tonight mademoiselle," the waiter commented. I didn't bother to say thank you just by the look on Sean's face. "What the hell is your problem," I asked.

He totally ignored me and flipped open his Sidekick. I grabbed it putting it in my purse. "After all your shit I put up with and you disrespect me like this. I'm not Tasha or any of those other bitches that you mess around with. As a matter of fact I'm not even hungry anymore; have dinner by your damn self."

"Are you done," he asked nonchalantly. "Yes I'm done. Why did you have to spoil a perfectly good evening?" "Can I have my Sidekick back please?" I threw it at him and stormed out of there leaving him to catch his own ride back to Miami Beach.

I drove around hating myself for going back on my word. I should have never come back to Miami or allowed myself to think I could be happy with him again. I ended up at the beach to listen to the waves crashing into each other. I needed a place of solitude to recollect my thoughts. I knew when I got home it would be hell to pay for walking out and leaving him.

Sean ordered dinner to go for two and had the restaurant call him a taxi. He tried calling me on my cell phone but I didn't answer. He knew he was wrong but his pride wouldn't let him apologize. He was praying I was there when he arrived. He didn't want me to leave upset with him because not knowing where I was would not be his only problem.

The taxi pulled in the driveway; there was no sign of my truck. He immediately started blowing up my phone. He didn't like me being out at night by myself. It was eleven at night and there was still no answer. He paced the floors back and forth until he heard a car pull up. He waited for me to turn the knob so that he could tell me what a fool he had been. Tommy walked in with cases of Coronas and Heinekens.

"What's up son?" "I thought you were my girl." "Where she at? It's getting late," Tommy said looking at his watch. "We had a fight and she left me at the restaurant." "And you made it home before her? You must have really pissed her off." "I did." "Son, check this out; I heard Tasha is in the hospital all swollen up like a sumo wrestler."

"She got what she deserved; she'll think twice before she puts another man's babies on someone else. On the real, I think Angel's pregnant. Her breasts are big as hell and you know how flat her stomach always is; she has this cute little budge that could be my son or daughter." "So why you starting trouble with her; getting her all upset and stressed out." "We made love all day long and I'll be a man and admit it, she had a nigga's head all messed up.

When she told me she was still leaving I got really nasty with it. I should have never allowed her to leave that restaurant yet alone ride off at night by herself in a car that she's never driven before. I'm obsessed with that girl and I can't get use to living without her."

I walked in the door at one in the morning. Sean and Tommy were waiting up for me.

"What's up Tommy?" "What's up baby girl?" "Where you been? I've been calling your phone all night," Sean said getting in my face. Tommy got up and pulled him back. "Oh, you're talking to me now." He took my cell phone and looked at the screen. "You don't see this; it says twenty-one missed calls." "We're not together anymore. I don't have to answer to you or your calls if I don't want to.

You have to learn to separate your personal and business life. Our life is not your stage; you're not performing in front of millions of people here it's just me. I'm not going to let you treat me any kind of way and when you're over your tantrums you want me to forget all the hurtful things you did and said to me.

Hellll No!" "All I'm saying is that I was worried about you and you could have answered to let me know you were alright. You know how much I love you and I'm so sorry for the way I behaved." "I'm sorry too baby. I should have been more sensitive to your feelings and I especially shouldn't have left you in that restaurant. It could have been a crazed fan or reporter there waiting to blow the story out of proportion.

Will you forgive me?" "I always forgive you; now go upstairs and take your clothes off." "Is that all you think about?" "I'm making up for lost time. I brought you some eggplant lasagna; it's in the fridge." I warmed up my lasagna and shared a plate with Tommy. He was like the brother I never had and there was nothing that we couldn't or didn't talk about.

"I haven't seen you much since I've been here. What's been going on with you? Any new romances?" "I'm too busy dealing with ya'll drama." "I'm sorry." "Nah it's cool. It was this one girl that I met in Orlando. She was cool at first until she found out who I was and what I did. She starts asking for money and wanting to go on shopping sprees like everyday. Can you believe this girl asked me to buy her an Ashton Martin? I don't even drive an Ashton Martin!"

"Tommy stop lying. How long were you guys dating?" "About six months; check this out that's not even the worst part about it. I took her down to Jamaica for the weekend and we were about to do our thing but I didn't have any protection so you know I wasn't down with that. She was like; no don't worry about it I brought some. You know how I pay close attention to every detail so I go to get a condom out of the already opened box and she had poked these tiny needle holes in every one.

I put that bitch on a flight the next morning and before her flight had a chance to land my number was changed." "Did you give her a chance to explain?" "What's to explain you just tried to trap me into getting you pregnant? When you find girls like that leave them where they at; those are the same bitches that will try to bring you up on rape charges."

"Maybe that's why industry only dates industry or money only marries money but I guess there are some rare cases where someone in the public eye finds that regular person that just loves them for them." "Maybe one day I'll be lucky enough to find someone that loves me the way you love Sean." "Just promise me when you do you won't take her for granted and make sure you never deprive her of your affection.

Affection is all a woman really wants. When a man treats a woman like she's the only woman in the world; his queen, his mother and his daughter. There's nothing in this world or the world to come that we won't do for you. That's why your boy over there is such a spoiled brat." "If I was spoiled you would stay and never leave me," Sean said throwing his two cents in.

Tommy and I finished eating and I offered to clean our dishes. "It's cool sis I got it," Tommy said kissing me on my cheek. I walked around to the media room where Sean was deeply involved in a game of Madden. "Can I play with you?" "Yeah come on let me put this beat down on you. Where's Tommy? Did he leave?" "No. He's in the kitchen." "Call him over the intercom and have him bring me another Corona."

I called Tommy to bring a case of Coronas and slices of lime for Sean and myself. "You know better. You're not drinking while you're pregnant and have my baby come out retarded. Call Tommy back and tell him to go to the store and pick you up an EPT Test." "I'm not asking him to do that. I really wish you would lay off this pregnancy thing."

"If it's nothing to worry about, then you won't have a problem taking the test." Tommy walked in with the requested items and Sean demanded that he go out for the test. He swore it was no way I was leaving until I took the test and found out once and for all if I was carrying his second child but, this one we would keep. I went into a state of panic and he sensed that something was wrong. He put down the game control and knelt down in front of me.

"There's something you're not saying." "I'm not ready for a baby right now." "Why not? I thought this is what you wanted; what we wanted." "Yeah; when we were engaged to be married. I'm not trying to be a single parent." "Why would you have to be? I'm not going anywhere." He took my hands into his.

"In my world you are already my wife but let's make it official; marry me?" "Sean I can't make that decision right now." "At least put your ring back on." "It wouldn't mean the same. A lot has changed from the day you placed it on my finger. When I saw you making love to another woman my heart stopped. I know you think my coming here means I'm over it, but let the truth be told I will never forget. It's like a mental movie that plays in my mind the same time everyday.

You said you were in love with me and only me. What happened to our promises to ride or die for one another no matter what?" "I'm so in love with you that if the death angel came for you I would make a deal with God to take me instead. I just wanna make things right between us again."

The tears fell from our eyes for different reasons. For him; hurting me for the years of unfaithfulness. For me; knowing that this kind of hurt would never heal.

"Where do we go from here," he asked. "I don't know. It hurts too much to love you." He buried his head in my lap and sobbed like he had lost his last friend. By instinct I wanted to comfort and console him but I was the one confused and broken hearted. I sat there thinking how rich and unhappy we were. All envied us and at that moment I wished I could trade places with them.

Tommy came in with a grocery bag full of every brand of pregnancy test on the shelf. "What happened; somebody died," Tommy asked thinking that Tasha had sustained injuries that had taken her out of here. "Everyone is fine just give us a minute," I said.

Tommy left the bag on the floor and walked out of the room. "You and my mother are the only women that have seen me all venerable and exposed. Don't think I'm a punk for crying like this."

"Why would I think that?" "Because I'm a man." "And men can't cry. Your hurts and frustrations have to go somewhere or else they build up to the point that when they do come out you won't be able to control them."

"You're so good to me girl, always giving me words of wisdom and encouragement. A man needs a woman who understands his struggles, his hustle, his dreams and his fears without nagging a nigga to death."

"My mother groomed me at an early age to respect my man and let him be a man no matter what. When I was little, I wondered why mommy never let our maid wash my daddy's clothes or cook his food. When I got older and asked her why she had done that she said 'If you don't use anything else I taught you remember this; never allow your man to depend on another woman for anything.'

I miss her especially at times like these." "She was the finest mom I'd ever seen. She always wore the latest designer fashions even when she was cleaning the house. She was in a class all by herself. If your dad wasn't so damn cool I would have stolen your mom away from him." "Don't make me hurt you." "I'm just playing," he said with a hug.

"Seriously your dad exposed me to that life of the rich and famous before I even had a dime to my name. I had no idea that white wines compliment seafood or red wines compliment certain pasta dishes or which wines I should choose with my desserts. He taught me how to separate a good cigar from a great cigar just by the smell. You know it was because of him I invested my first royalty check. I stuck to your dad like glue inhaling everything he said and did because I saw how you adored him and I figured if I could be half the man he was you would never leave me." "He really loved you and thought of you as more than my boyfriend but a son.

They say a man always wants a son but after me my dad told mommy he was done because he could never love another child as much as he loved me. They made sure I never got lonely. I was involved in everything and we traveled all around the world that I didn't have time to long for a brother or sister. Remember when we first met and I was leaving for Hawaii and I begged my parents to let you come. We had the time of our lives." "Yeah, I'll never forget that trip." "You shouldn't; you took my virginity."

"I don't recall taking anything you gave it to me." "You've been hooked every since. I was scared straight into keeping my virginity because most of my friends and fast ass cousin was sexing since they were twelve and thirteen. They were like at first it's gonna be hard for him to get it in and when he does you start bleeding and you might even cry because it hurts so bad." "Did I hurt you?" "A little but it wasn't that bad." Our first time was nothing like I was told it would be. Before we undressed he asked me a million times if I was sure of what I wanted and if I was any other girl he would of just hit it and been done with it but he said I was special.

No boy had seen me naked before so I was hesitant about undressing in front of him. When my last piece of clothing fell to the floor he stood there examining every part of me. I covered myself with my hands thinking something was wrong. He moved closer to me and put my hands by my side. He said I was even perfect naked.

He laid me down and told me it was our wedding night because when I met him I told him I wasn't having sex until I was married. He told me if I relaxed it wouldn't hurt that much. Every inch that he slowly put in he asked if he was hurting me. I was happy that it was over though and I had shared my first sexual experience with him. I thought when we got back to Miami he would forget about what we shared in Hawaii and me but he did the complete opposite.

When we returned home and back to school I tried to avoid him by not taking his calls and walking pass him in the halls and not saying a word. It wasn't until he blocked my parking space in the school's parking lot and asked me if he had done something wrong. I explained to him that I knew he was a player and I assumed that what happened in Hawaii stayed in Hawaii. He swore on his mother's life that he meant every word. From that day we were inseparable.

If I wasn't at his house he was at mine. He went on my family vacations and I spent summers with him when he went to visit his mom in New York. "How many girls had you slept with before me?" "About ten." "Before you were thirteen or playing hide and go get doesn't count. You know how you guys always say 'I lost my virginity when I was eight'."

"Wait a minute; you didn't grow up in the hood how do you know about hide and go get?" "When I would go to Tasha's house; one day she dragged me down the block to play hide and go get. I had heard of hide and seek but hide and go get was something new to me. When she told me what it was I was like ya'll are nasty I'm telling.

Those kids hated me and they told Tasha not to be friends with her own cousin because every time they asked me to play I ran in the house to tell my aunt." "You know I was a PIMP before you snatched me up. I had all the girls on lock in that school and when they found out you was my girl; they were sick."

"I always wondered why they hated me so much. Men and women are different in that way. If you're dating a man that women want they will hate on you long after you two have broken up but a man will give you props all day long for having a dime piece on your arm." "As long as I'm breathing I will never understand you women." "That's the beauty of us the suspense." Sean stood up and handed me a pregnancy test. "You ready to get this over with. We need to know so you can start your check ups."

I couldn't think of any excuses to get out of this. A part of me wanted to know because I would feel guilty if my baby was sick and I neglected its health for my own selfish reasons. I agreed to take the test not for him or me but for what could be our unborn child. I went to the bathroom around the corner and locked the door behind me. I followed the instructions and waited for the results. I sat there thinking that in an instant I could be someone's mother. I looked at the results and Sean had been right along. I was pregnant with his child. There was no sense of hiding the results because he was anxiously waiting outside of the door.

I opened the door trying not to look too excited. "Well," he said waiting for my answer. I stood there shaking my head. His excitement instantly turned to disappointment. "Congratulations daddy!" "Yes, I knew it," he said picking me up. Tommy came around the corner carrying my cell phone. "Your phone has been ringing non-stop." I answered hearing my aunt's broken voice on the other end.

"Auntie slow down I can't understand a word you're saying." "Tasha's been hurt really bad and she's at Jackson Memorial. I know you girls are going through difficult times but we are still family. I think it would help if you were the voice she heard when she woke up." "Yes of course auntie; I'm on my way." I dropped the phone and looked at Sean. "Tasha's been hurt. My aunt says it's really bad."

Tommy and Sean looked at each other like they already knew. "Where are you going," Sean asked. "I have to go to her. Even though she treated me like shit I can't do her the same way." "I thought we were going to celebrate." "Celebrate what," Tommy asked. "She's pregnant and I'm not going to let anyone stress you out." "I'm happy for you two. He's right sis you should be celebrating at a time like this not dealing with outside drama." "I love you guys for caring and respect what you're saying but I already promised my aunt I would be there." "If you must go let Tommy drive you."

I slipped on my shoes, kissed Sean good-bye and walked out the door with Tommy. Nothing Tommy said gave me comfort. I couldn't imagine what had happened because my aunt had not given me that information. "Can you drive any faster?" "Sean would kill me if he knew I was driving like a maniac with you in the car."

It took us thirty minutes to get there. I asked Tommy to drop me off but he insisted on staying and walking upstairs to her room with me. When the elevator door opened my aunt was the first face I saw. It had been a while since I'd seen her that I couldn't wait to run to her and wrap my arms around her. "I'm so glad that you decided to come. You get more beautiful each time I see you." I introduced Tommy and she walked us around to Tasha's room.

Tommy and I walked in hand and hand. "You sure you can handle this." "I have you here, you'll make everything alright." If it hadn't been for her name tattooed on her neck I would have never known it was her. They had her hooked up to several machines and tubes were coming out of everywhere. I broke down and fell into Tommy's arms. "Let me take you home. You don't need to do this right now." I agreed only if he left me alone to talk to her. He promised to stand right outside of the door and give me all the time I needed. I pulled a chair next to her bed and grabbed her hand.

She couldn't open her eyes but once I told her who I was she squeezed my hand. I asked her not to try and speak just to let me pure my heart out. I told her how sorry I was this happened to her and how I never stopped loving her. I even told her how I wanted to come back in the restaurant that day and help her work through her pain. A tear fell from her left eye. She tried to speak but the tube they had down her throat stopped her from doing so. I

116

kissed her on her forehand and told her I would see her tomorrow. She squeezed my hand even harder as to say 'don't go.'

I had to call Monica and tell her what happened and let her know I would be here for a few more days. Tommy and I kissed my aunt before returning to the elevator and I told her I would return on tomorrow. Tommy and I were both speechless on the drive home. I called out to Sean as soon as I walked in the house. He was upstairs talking to his mother. "She just walked in; I'll let you talk to her." He handed me the phone and went out to talk to Tommy. "Was it as bad as you heard," Sean asked. "Worst. You can't even recognize her." "Damn. How did Angel take it?" "Not too good," Tommy said wishing he had not allowed Sean to have her jumped.

"What's on my schedule for tomorrow?" "You have meetings and conference calls all morning and you have to approve the artwork for the new album." "Reschedule my calls until next week and you take my meetings and have David bring the artwork first thing in the morning. I'm taking her away tomorrow." "Cool; I'll crash in the guest bedroom."

They gave one another dap and walked off into different directions. When Sean walked into the room I was lying on the bed still talking to his mother. He lay next to me rubbing and kissing my stomach. I wrapped up my conversation with his mother and promised I wouldn't let weeks pass without calling. I hung up the phone and filled Sean in on Tasha's condition.

"They suspect it's someone she knows because they went straight in for her and didn't take a thing. I've never seen someone so black and blue. She couldn't even open her eyes." "Karma is a bitch." "That wasn't nice." "It wasn't meant to be. Why would you care after everything she did to you; to us?" "The same reason why I'm here with you. I can't just stop loving someone because they made a mistake or two." "I have a surprise for you." "Baby I already have too much and not to mention you just bought me a new car today."

"When I found out you were pregnant I called my realtor about showing us a few properties in Atlanta. We're flying out tomorrow afternoon." "I can't fly to Atlanta tomorrow; I have too much to do." "I'm not taking no for an answer besides your ticket is already booked." "Don't you think you should consult me before you make plans for me?"

When we were together I thought it was romantic how he would plan surprise get a ways but for the first time I was annoyed that he would assume that living in Atlanta with him was still something I dreamed about and that he was totally avoiding the fact I was trying to leave. I could only imagine how my life would be once I had his baby; complete lock down with the keys no where in sight. I had to find a way to leave when he least expected it because if he had to say good-bye it was guaranteed drama. I didn't need his gifts but anything he wanted to do for our child I had to honor it so I agreed to fly to Atlanta with him.

He kissed me on my forehead and promised I wouldn't be sorry. I pulled out my *Louis Vuitton* roll on luggage and packed enough for two days. "You can't pack for me anymore?" "You know how you do; I just assumed you were going shopping when you got there." "I probably won't go near any malls my main focus is finding us the perfect house."

I went to his closet to get his Gucci Bags that were still packed from his last trip. He never unpacked he always left that up to Tommy or myself. I unpacked his clothes and placed them in the bag to go out to the cleaners. I picked out his clothes and shoes and repacked his bags. "Ha beautiful, come over here," he said lying in the bed. I walked over and got under the sheets with him.

He slipped off my gown and panties taking off his boxers and throwing them to the floor. "I just want to hold you like this tonight." We kissed good night and fell asleep with our hands intertwined. It was three in the morning when my cell phone woke me up. I hated those in the middle of the night calls; for me that meant something was wrong. I answered with butterflies in my stomach.

"Hello," I answered in a low voice. "Angel." "Gene," I whispered not wanting Sean to hear me. "I haven't heard from you and I went by the condo and no one was there. I've been worried sick about you. Are you okay?" I had been completely honest with him concerning Sean's and I relationship so I felt at ease about telling him where I was. "I'm fine. Sean was in trouble so I had to fly back to Miami.

I'm sorry you were worried; I left so fast I didn't have time to see you and let you know I was leaving. How have you been?" "Missing you, how long are you there for?" "Aaah, I miss you too." "Who's that," Sean said waking up. I put my hand on the receiver and whispered. "My friend." He reached over to snatch the phone from my hand. I tried to get up and he grabbed my arm and took the phone from me. "Sean, please don't do this. This has nothing to do with you." "You're carrying my baby so this has everything to do with me."

That's exactly why I didn't want him to know I was pregnant. All I could do was sit there and listen to him go off on the man I was trying to start over with. I begin to cry hysterically when the words I dreaded came out of his mouth straight to Gene's ears. "The only reason she would allow you close to her is because I wasn't there. You don't have to worry about her anymore because that's me, all me. I'd be damn if I let another man raise my child."

"Child, what child," Gene asked being informed of what I wanted to tell him. "Oh you didn't know she was having my baby." He didn't either until last night but he had to take any cheap shot he could knowing that my feelings that once only belonged to him was shared with the man on the other end. "That doesn't change my feelings for her that just means she's going to really need me now. I don't have a problem with a child I didn't father calling me daddy."

I could see and hear the anger in his voice but I felt he deserved everything that was being said to him for bombarding himself into my conversation. "All I'm telling you partner is whatever it is you're selling my girl's not buying." He finally noticed me crying and hung up the phone. I pulled the covers over my head hoping he wouldn't say anything to me but that only pissed him off more. He pulled the covers back and let me have everything he didn't give to Gene.

"Why were you talking to another man in our house? Do you know how disrespectful that is?" "He called me." "At three in the morning?" "You're an asshole. Did you really have to go there with him? Have I ever gone off on any of those females you were screwing around with? You act like I'm sleeping with him. You had no right to tell him I was pregnant; that wasn't your place." "If you think for one second you're going to have my baby around this dude you better think twice." "If you keep blowing up like this you're the one who won't be around our child."

"Angel, don't ever play with me like that." "Do you realize how stupid you sound? The baby isn't even here yet; you should be praying that I deliver a healthy child." I got up threw my robe on and walked out the room. I went to the office and locked the door behind me. I wrestled with the idea of calling him back or just letting it ride. My feelings were too deep to leave him wondering and confused. I took a deep breath and pressed redial.

"Angel, what's going on over there? He was pretty upset did he touch you?" "No. He would never hit me." "He was a real jerk. I'm sorry to have caused so much trouble." "I can't let you take the blame; he's just having a hard time with me moving on. I have to be honest with you; I found out yesterday that I was pregnant and I would completely understand if you wanted to walk away." "When you found out did your feelings change for me?" "No, actually you were the first person I thought about. I knew once I told you I would lose you before I even had you."

"You will never lose me. You had me the first time we danced. I have this incredible amount of admiration for you that you would trust me with your feelings after he hurt you so bad." "I'm so ready to come back home. If I had it my way I would have left days ago." "Hurry back and take care of yourself." "So I'll see you soon," I said wondering why I had left peace for a storm.

I went to the kitchen to cut up some mangoes and strawberries. I put in a movie and lay on the sofa thinking about what a loose cannon I was dealing with. It was the first time Sean had beef with any guy because of me and I was still shocked by the confrontation that had taken place between them. What the hell was I doing here?

Maybe I was leading him on by still sleeping with him but what was a girl to do; the shit was the bomb. I really needed to talk to Monica but I knew she was knocked out by this time. I called her anyway and gave her the good news about the baby. She was more excited than me. I filled her in about my hospital visit to see Tasha and tried to put into words how she looked. I vented about me not being able to prevent Sean from going off on Gene.

"I told you not to go see that nut. He would've been all right; he and his people have to learn to get by without you. When are you coming back?" "He wants me to fly to Atlanta tomorrow." "For what?" "He wants to buy another house." "The longer you stay the harder it's going to be to leave. You do know that's his plan, right?" "I know." "And now that he knows you're pregnant your ass is involved in some Jerry Springer drama."

"You won't believe what I'm pushing while I'm here." "What?" "The new Benz Truck that's not even available in the U.S. yet." "How did they let him take that on a test drive?" "He bought it for me and had it shipped; it arrived yesterday." "You're kidding." "No, I'm not kidding. It's top of the line black on black with a diamond-crusted nameplate that says 'Sean's wife.' I'm still trying to figure out how everything works."

"You can not leave that car there." "You know he did that on purpose. He knew it would be hard for me to depart from this car." "Where is he anyway?" "Somewhere upstairs, sleeping I hope." "Don't let him aggravate you too much because that baby is going to come out looking just like him." "I'll see you in a few days and try not to have too much fun without me." "I love you and have a safe flight." "I love you too; goodnight." I was so tired but I refused to sleep next to him so I fell asleep on the sofa.

Sean woke up and I still hadn't come to bed. He paged me but I was sound asleep unknown to him. All kinds of thoughts ran through his mind. He wouldn't blame me for leaving after the way he blew things out of proportion. He searched every room until he found me balled up like a baby on the sofa. He wondered if he was the one I still dreamed about when I closed my eyes.

He picked me up and carried me back upstairs. He wrapped my arms around his neck and laid my head on his shoulder. He put me back to bed and lay down next to me. "I love you so much," he said kissing my hand. He wanted to hide me away from the world to have me all to himself but with Gene now in the picture it was too late.

Tasha opened her eyes and reached out for Dre. It was as if she had been in a coma and was unaware of her surroundings. She tried removing her tubes and the IV they placed in her arm. Dre took one hand and her mother took the other while Dre pushed the nurse's button. They agreed the swelling in Tasha's face had begun to go down so they were able to remove her tube.

The doctor informed them that besides her sprung ankle everything else looked good and they would be sending her home tomorrow. "The police officer said once you were awake and able to speak you needed to come to the station and officially make a statement," Dre said. "I'm not making any statements. I just want to forget this ever happened and go on with what's left of my life."

"If I have to drag your butt down there myself you will make a statement and press charges to the fullest extinct of the law. What if this happens again and you're not so lucky." "Mommy it won't happen again." "How can you be so sure? Do you know something you're not saying?" In the back of her mind she knew Sean had something to do with this. After everything he did for her and the kids and to find out they were not his would send anybody over the edge. If all she got was a beat down from some females she was gladly willing to accept that.

"I don't know anything; it was probably just some jealous girls from around the way." "From now on you stay away from Roxanne's house until they find out who did this," Dre demanded. "Those are my people over there. I'm not going to let some haters run me away." "Your people almost killed you. I know you're grown but I'm still your mother and I'm putting my foot down; you are to stay away from there. If Roxanne wants to see you I'm sure she won't have a problem driving to Ft. Lauderdale," her mother said with authority.

She knew she was not winning this argument so she agreed and gave in. "Mommy, I had a dream that Angel was here last night." "It wasn't a dream baby it was real. Her and this nice young man stopped by. You should give her a call; she was so worried last night." "What would I say it's been so much tension between us lately?" "You'll find the words; honesty always wins out in the end."

She reached for the phone and called her cousin. She was not expecting Sean to answer my cell phone. She was so caught off guard that he said hello three times before she said anything. "Is Angel around?" He recognized that voice. "Tasha? I can't believe you would have the audacity to even call this phone." "I feel so bad about this whole thing. I honestly didn't know." "Sure you didn't.

When I first found out I was devastated and really wanted to hurt you but what the devil took away from me God blessed me with.

Angel is pregnant and I don't need you calling her with your issues and problems jeopardizing my baby's health because then I will hurt you." She felt like a fool for flaunting her kids in my face and in the end it turned out that I would be the woman to give him his first child after all.

"Will you at least let her know I will be discharged tomorrow," she asked before she realized he had already hung up.

"Were you able to reach her," her mother asked. "Sean wouldn't allow me to speak to her." "What do you mean he wouldn't allow you? He can't control that." "You don't know him. He can and he will. Now that she's pregnant he will never let me close to her again." "At this point I can only offer advice because you made your own bed as far as that boy's concerned but Angel is my niece; my dead sister's only child and I will be damned if I'm going to let anyone keep me from her."

"You're welcome to call but as for me I'm not calling anymore." "I'm sure she'll call you; in the mean time try and get some rest," her mother said leaving the room. Dre and Tasha's mother left for Ft. Lauderdale to prepare for Tasha and the kids to move in permanently. Dre had Roxanne meet them at his house so that they could go shopping while he painted and decorated the rooms for his daughters. He refused to bring anything in his house that Sean had purchased including their wardrobe that was worth thousands of dollars. He painted Shawna and Shanice's room pink mist with white colored roses and Chanel and Chantel's room lavender with white lilies.

Once Tasha was released they would sit the children down and try to explain to them that the man they knew as daddy was no more and that this would be their new home. He knew kids were resilient but them having to go from calling him Dre to daddy right away would be too much for them to bare. He thanked God they found out the results while they were still young because as time passed they would forget that they had ever called another man daddy.

I woke up to breakfast in bed. Sean had fixed me a plate of French toast and a bowl of fresh picked berries. I got up washed my face and brushed my teeth before eating. "Why can't you be this sweet all the time?" "I am but you just drive me so crazy." "Come join me I can't eat all of this. Did you bring me upstairs last night?" "I wasn't about to let you sleep on the sofa all night."

"I didn't want to sleep there either but I was too upset with you to come back up. Honestly, how does it feel when the shoe is on the other foot?" "It feels like hell. Especially when he told me he was in love with you." "He told you that he was in love with me?" He noticed my over excitement and refused to answer the question.

"What time does our flight leave?" "Around 3:00. I made a doctor's appointment for you this morning." "What time do we have to be there?" "In an hour so hurry and get ready." "Come shower with me." "Uh uh," he said shaking his head. "Why not?" "You know why. My intentions are totally different from yours right now."

I showered alone and dressed in a strapless sundress. Sean loaded the luggage in the car because we would go from the doctor directly to the airport. It was freezing when we walked into the doctor's office so Sean went back to the car to get my shawl. "Are you nervous," he asked. "A little, I'm more excited than anything else. I hope they will be able to tell the sex of the baby." "I want a boy." "And if it's a girl, then what?" "Either way I'm happy but if it's a girl we'll keep trying until we make a boy." "You can keep trying but it won't be with me because this is it."

The lady sitting next to us joined in on the conversation. "I know that's right. That's the same thing I told my husband." We both laughed but Sean didn't find it funny at all. "How many months are you?" "I don't know; this is our first doctor's visit." "How far along are you?" "Six months and counting down the days." "Is it that bad?"

"For me it has been. I was little just how you are right now and look at me now. The worst part for me is when my baby gets right under my ribs; that's the most annoying feeling. And make sure you invest in a lot of Tums because the heartburn is non-stop." The doctor called us back just when she was getting to the good parts. "That's us; it was nice talking to you." "You too and good luck." "Thank you," Sean and I said as we walked to the back.

The nurse handed me a cup for a urine sample. When that was done they pricked my finger for blood samples, took my weight and blood pressure. They asked when my last menstrual cycle was but Sean nor could I remember. They took us to a room where I was told to undress and put on the gown provided for me. The doctor knocked before coming in with the nurse.

"Your pregnancy test was positive and your iron looks really good but today we're going to do a vaginal exam, ultra sound and listen to the heart beat or heartbeats." "Will you be able to determine the sex of the baby," Sean asked. "If she's far along enough." The nurse instructed me to put my feet in the stirrups. I hated vaginal exams and those stirrups that had to be created by a man. This was the first time Sean had accompanied me to my gynecologists and witnessed a vaginal exam.

He was totally freaked out about the whole thing. "That doesn't hurt her," he squirmed. "It shouldn't hurt just a little discomfort," Dr. Green responded. "You may experience slight bleeding due to the scraping of your cervix but it's nothing to be alarmed by." Dr. Green told me to get dressed and come to the room across the hall where the ultrasound would be performed.

Sean and I were both anxious to find out what we were having. I wrapped a sheet around myself and pulled my dress up over my stomach. She put cold gel on my stomach and turned on the machine. She checked the measurements, the body parts and the fluid surrounding the baby. "It's only one baby. The baby is measuring about eighteen weeks. So you are about four and a half months pregnant." "Are you sure I'm that far along? I'm not even showing yet." "All women carry their babies differently. You may be small now but in a few weeks or months you could have a big beach ball sitting on your lap.

Do you guys want to know what you're having?" When she moved to the right the baby moved to the left when she moved to the left the baby moved to the right. We laughed at how our baby already had its little personality. "If the baby keeps moving I won't be able to tell." I put my hand on the right side of my stomach and talked to my baby for the first time. "You have to stay still so mommy and daddy can find out what you are and give you a name." The baby immediately stopped moving as if it had heard me.

"It looks like you're having a boy." Tears were already preserved in Sean's eyes but when she told us it was a boy they poured from his eyes like rain. "Oh baby," I said wiping his tears away. The sonogram tech wiped the gel away and told me to stop at the front desk for my appointment. They provided me with prenatal vitamins and scheduled me for a three-week check up. Sean was still crying when we reached the car. "Baby what's wrong?"

"You've made me so happy and seeing you talk to him the way you did in there just blew my mind. I couldn't love you more than I do at this moment." "I can't believe I'm almost five months pregnant. I had to have gotten pregnant when we went to Barbados for Valentine's Day." "I have to call my mother; she's going to loose her mind. Do you know every time I speak to her she asks when am I going to have her some grandbabies?" "She asks me the exact same thing. Why don't we fly up from Atlanta and surprise her?" "She was just saying if she wanted to see you she would have to fly to Miami."

Chapter Eleven

When we arrived at the airport it was hectic as usual. Miami International was especially crowded in the summer months with all the celebrities and tourists vacationing. We unloaded our baggage and went straight to the counter. The gentleman at the reservations counter recognized Sean and called us an escort to personally take us to our plane. I stood there for ten minutes while he signed autographs for everyone. The flight attendant allowed us to board first class before anyone else. Having celebrity status definitely had its perks and advantages. As soon as I boarded the plane I reached for a blanket, let my seat back, and closed my eyes. I could hear words coming out of Sean's mouth but I was so sleepy that I couldn't make them out. I fell asleep half way into the flight.

A guy that he knew from back home spotted him. "Sean?" "Rob?" "What's up Son? Where you at now?" "I'm still in Miami." "You still in New York?" "Hell yeah. I'm never leaving that place."

Rob was a rapper trying to get signed when Sean moved to Miami. A major label had just picked him up and he asked Sean if he would do sixteen bars on the track he was recording in Atlanta. They exchanged numbers and Sean agreed to meet up and listen to the track that would be his debut single. He knew with Sean being a multi platinum artist it would be a guaranteed hit. Sean woke me up just as we were about to land. Against the advice of the pilot to stay in our seats my bladder was about to explode and I just had to make a run for the restroom. When I got to Atlanta it was so many black people. Nothing like South Beach, Miami Beach had such a rainbow of people. The first time I visited I fell in love with the place. It seemed as if the African Americans had all the money, power and respect. It was nothing to go out and see celebrities walking around without bodyguards. Atlanta was truly Black Hollywood. After getting our bags we took a limo to pick up our rental car. Sean called his real estate agent to find out what time we were linking up.

He bragged about how we were going to love the houses he had selected. Sean informed him that we were staying at *The Ritz Carlton* and he could fax over the properties that were already found for pre-approval. I wasn't hungry but Sean insisted that I eat so we drove to *The Cheesecake Factory*. I ordered The Oriental Chicken Salad and he ordered Scrimp Scampi without the garlic. We talked and laughed like we were in high school again. It felt good at that moment to live in a perfect world.

I excused myself to the restroom and ordered two slices of carrot cake to go, on my way back to the table. Several girls were crowded around Sean taking pictures with their camera phones and asking him to leave his signature anywhere he pleased. As I sat down he introduced me as his wife and continued posing for pictures. It never bothered me that everyone wanted a piece of him. It was the women and sometimes even the men that would roll their eyes and talk shit about what he was doing with me when he could have all of them.

They would be so gone that they would actually try to fight me and believed that just because they had every album, went to every concert, and read everything that was ever written about him they were entitled to him. If they were half the women they thought they were they would've been thanking me for allowing them to have those dreams and fantasies. I could have been one of those jealous artists' girls that never let them do anything when they were around. After all, they were the reason we could afford the biggest houses, drive the finest cars, travel all over the world and live life like it was suppose to be lived. The waitress brought out the bill and a complementary strawberry cheesecake.

He paid the bill left a big tip, *as usual*, and walked out handing our ticket to valet. We drove down Peachtree Street heading towards our hotel. We checked into our executive suite and the receptionist handed him a thick manila folder. It was at least thirty pages of houses with pictures and descriptions. We went to our suite and divided the pages equally amongst ourselves.

He found about five possible and I only found two. I called Mike and gave him the MLS numbers on the ones we had chosen. We agreed that he would come to the hotel in an hour so that we could ride with him. I undressed and stood in front of the mirror looking at how my figure was slowing changing. Sean came in and stood behind me with both of his manicured hands touching my stomach.

"Oh shit; did you feel that?" "I did."

That was the first time I felt my baby move inside of me. God hadn't created words to describe what that felt like. He turned me around and looked straight into my gray eyes.

"Thank You. I will never disappoint you or our son. I put that on everything I own." "You're a good man." I showered and walked out with nothing on hoping to entice him into a quickie. He obliged but it was different.

"What's wrong?" "I don't wanna hurt the baby." I wanted him to put it on me like he just got home from a six-month tour.

"Come on, you won't hurt him." "Maybe we should consult your doctor first." "Whatever," I said pushing him off of me. "Don't be upset with me." "I don't get upset I get even." "Come on mommy, don't be that way." I dressed in the sexiest outfit I could find and teased him by slowly taking it off only to dress in the original outfit I planned to wear.

"Damn mommy, why you gotta play with a nigga like that?" I grabbed my Chanel Bag and headed out the door. He pinched my nipple as we waited for the elevator. "Ouch that hurts," I said punching him in his arm. "Isn't that what you women want; foreplay?" "No. Not when we ain't getting any. That's like having the macaroni without the cheese."

The elevator finally came and we caught it downstairs. His phone rang just as we stepped out. "I can't talk right now." The person on the other line must have questioned him as to why. "I just can't. I'll call you later." "Who was that?" "A friend." I took my hand and mushed him in the face. "I'm through with you. Don't talk to me."

He hugged me so tight; I couldn't push away if I wanted to. It was nothing that turned me on more than a good smelling man. We waited at the bar until Mike arrived. Mike had really come up, last time I saw him he was pushing a Camry. I walked outside looking for that same old car until he pressed his keyless remote and a dark green Maybach beeped.

"This you right here son?" "Holla at a playa dawg." "Baby you here this nigga, holla at a playa. Your wife would kill your ass."

When these two got together they acted like straight fools.

"How long are you guys in town for?" "Until tomorrow," Sean said. "Angel you finally convinced him to buy a house here?" "This was all him." "Atlanta is one of the best cities to live and raise a family in. Don't get me wrong; Miami is beautiful but ya'll just get too many damn hurricanes." "How are Stacey and the kids?" "They're all spoiled rotten. I hear you're in the family way?" "Today we found out we're having a boy," I said smiling. "Congratulations, how many more do you want?" "Four." "None." Sean and I said at the same time. "Mike, I need you to settle this debate for us. When Stacey was pregnant did the doctor allow you guys to still have sexual intercourse?"

"Hell yeah, that's the best sex ever. No offense Angel, but you don't have to worry about getting them pregnant because they already are." "I don't know about all of that, but thank you for schooling your boy," I said happy that someone else agreed with me. "Cool", he said giving me his, ' it's on' look. "We'll start off with the properties that are the farthest and work our way down."

We drove to *Gwinnett County* off of Sugarloaf Parkway. The mansions were breathtaking but almost identical to the ones back home. The only things missing were the palm trees and the Mediterranean roofs. Sean wanted something where the neighbors would be miles apart. I wanted to see them anyway to get an idea of what we would be getting for our money. One of the things I hated about him was how he spent money. He never compared prices yet alone asked about them.

I found it the perfect time to ask when Mike got out, *to unlock the lock box.* "What's our budget?" "I'll know when you find the house you fall in love with." "I'm not getting out of this car until you set one." "Fine ten million." "That's too much to spend on a house that's not our primary residence." "Ten Million and that's final."

He got out walked to the other side opened my door and we walked in the mansion together. It was nice but nothing to write home about. No matter where mansions were located the only difference was the architectural design and they were all guaranteed to have the big columns, marble or mahogany wood floors, winding marble staircases and beautiful crown molded ceilings. We saw two more houses in that neighborhood before heading back to the city. We pulled up to a black iron gate with a call box.

The owner's job had transferred him and his family to Japan and since Mike was the listing agent they had left him with the remote. "You're going to love this house." It took us about two minutes to reach the house from the gate. When we finally saw the house it was something out of a Disney Story Book. "How many acres is this?" "It's a little over seventeen."

Nothing could have prepared me for what was behind those glass doors. Mike gave us the grand tour of the first level and explained how all the marble was shipped from Italy, the fireplaces and the fountains were hand carved in Europe and the palm trees were brought over from Negril. Whenever we were in the market to buy a house we only dealt with Mike because he was a different kind of agent, not to pushy just to make a commission. He sat downstairs while he urged us to take our time and look around. The first room I wanted to see was the master bedroom and the closets.

The room was so huge that I could fit both the master bedrooms from our houses in Miami into this one room. I was sold on that room alone that I didn't need to go any farther. Sean came in and saw the excitement in my eyes. "Sean." "Shhh," he said putting his finger on my lips. "You don't have to say anything, it's yours." I took his face and kissed him passionately. "You know you're in trouble right?" "I know; punish me I've been a bad girl."

We laughed and walked downstairs to tell Mike what we had decided. "What did you two think?" "I'm speechless." "I knew you would love it." "What's the asking price," I asked knowing Sean could care less. "They want 12.5 but they are really anxious to sell because their paying a new mortgage plus the upkeep on this place and it's killing them." "We'll take it," Sean said. "Baby you just don't pay the price when there's room for negotiation," I said pulling him to the side. "Tell him we'll do 8.5 cash without repairs." "I'll call him right now."

Mike called Mr. Hudson and informed him he had a cash buyer for 8.5 million without having to fix or worry about checking up on the repairman's work since they were so far away. He counter offered at 9.5 without any repairs.

"I'll let my buyers know and you should be hearing from me by the end of the day." He walked over and gave us Mr. Hudson's counter offer. I thought that was a steal. It didn't matter that we had it. It was more to just buying a house. We could use those three million dollars for the repairs and furnishing the house because you didn't put any kind of furniture in a house this fabulous.

We left and went back to Mike's office where we signed the Purchase and Sale Agreement for the agreed upon price. Mike faxed the owner the contract in which he signed and immediately returned. It would be at least a week before he could return and hire movers. Mike brought out bottles of Cristal and Sparkling Grape Juice to celebrate. "You're playing with the big boys now," he said to Sean.

They made a toast to money and more money. I made a toast to God for choosing us to bless with the power to drop millions without blinking an eye. He never understood why I was so thrifty when I had grown up in such a wealthy family. Don't get me wrong, I splurged on designer clothes, bags and shoes, but I knew if I didn't respect what I was blessed with and worshiped material things over God, he would snatch it right from under me reminding me he was the one who even allowed me to have all that I had. It was almost in comparison to what happened to my cousin Louie.

He was sixteen and had a Benz to drive to school during the week and a Convertible Porsche to drive on the weekend. He had all kinds of jet skis and boats. My aunt even allowed him to move out of the main house into the guesthouse. He had and was given so much that he begin focusing on everything else but school. The day his father opened his report card and he was failing every subject including P.E., he went from driving to school to riding the bus. When the semester was over he was shipped off to a boarding school in England.

Mike and Sean dropped me off at Lenox Mall. Sean handed me his black card and told me to call him when I was ready. I would fly to Atlanta just for the malls. At Lenox Mall, all of my favorite designers are under one roof, *Louis Vuitton, Gucci, Dolce and Gabana, BCBG, Coach* and *Versace*. I went into the Louis Vuitton shop to see what new bags they had for the season.

I saw a bag I just couldn't live without so I ordered one for Monica and one for myself and requested that they be shipped to Miami. I passed by the Gucci store and had to go back when I eyed this briefcase that I knew he would love and ended up spending six thousand dollars on him but I put that on my platinum card. I wanted to buy the whole store up in BCBG but I didn't know how big I would get so, I only bought dresses. I spent five hundred dollars in Victoria Secret's buying lingerie and fragrances.

I felt my baby moving around so I walked to the food court and ordered some Sesame Tofu from the Chinese Restaurant. My mother said it wasn't good etiquette for a woman to eat everything off of her plate so I only ate half of it and threw the other away. I reached for my cell phone to let Sean know I was ready but my battery was dead. "I don't believe this." I looked in my purse for money to use the pay phone. Not even a dollar all I had was his black card and my platinum card because I had changed wallets before I left the hotel. It was a shame that I had millions in the bank but not even fifty cents to make a phone call.

Sean was in the studio recording the hook he promised to do for Rob. It was getting late so he stepped out the booth to check his messages. He was surprised I hadn't called yet so he called me instead. It went straight to my voice mail. He tried once more before going back. It was still going to voice mail so he left a message. "Baby, I'm in the studio with Rob. It's getting late and the mall should be closing soon so call me and let me know what time to be out there."

I thought about asking someone to let me use their cell phone but everybody looked like they didn't want to bothered. I went back to The Gucci Store to ask to use the phone since I had just spent thousands of dollars in there. "My cell phone just died and I really need to use your phone to call my ride." The salesman went over and said a few words to his manager. "We don't usually do this but we'll make this exception." "Thank You." I called Sean and it kept ringing until it went to his voicemail. "Sean, my cell phone is dead so I couldn't call but I'll be waiting outside." I thanked the man at the counter and walked outside to wait for my ride.

He finished his session and was just hanging out when his message alert sounded off. 'You have one unheard message.' "Sean, my cell phone is dead so I couldn't call but I'll be waiting outside." He came speeding through the front entrance an hour later. He jumped out to load the hundreds of bags; *that were surrounding me*, into the trunk. He put me in the car closed my door and drove away.

"Where were you?" "At the studio; you need to start charging your phone, anything could have happened to you and I would have never gotten over it." There was nothing I could say; he was right. "We got invited to a movie premiere tonight, you down?" "Would you be terribly upset if I stayed in tonight?" "I'm not going without you."

"Take Mike I can't go out tonight and get up in the morning and fly to New York." "You sure?" "Yes I'm sure; go and enjoy yourself but not too much." "What am I going to wear?" "I bought you some things from Gucci. Why don't you rock those?" He dressed in a black Gucci suit, white shirt and black Gucci shoes. 'Damn he was fine,' I thought to myself. I was glad that he belonged to me until I went back to The Bahamas.

He ordered jumbo shrimp and fruit from room service and we ate together before he left. "I love you girl," he said kissing me from my lips to my neck. "Okay don't start nothing you can't finish." "Who said I couldn't finish it, don't make me take these clothes off." "No, go have fun I'll be here when you get back," I said pushing him towards the door. "I went into the bathroom to run my bath and put aroma theory candles around to relax. I set the timer for an hour closed my eyes and went to sleep.

Mike met Sean at Atlantic Station where the premiere was being held. "You got shades," Sean asked him. "What do I need shades for its dark as hell." "When all those lights start hitting your ass it's going take days before you stop seeing spots." Mike pulled out some flimsy sunglasses. "You not wearing those are you?" "Yeah why not?" "Son, where did you get those from?"

"The Flea Market." Sean burst into laughter. "You're driving a Maybach and rocking some five dollar shades."

Sean pulled out a pair of his Dior Shades and handed them over. "There yours." "That's what's up," Mike said giving him some dap. When they reached the red carpet Mike had never seen so many people with cameras, recorders and microphones. "This is crazy," he whispered to Sean. "Welcome to my world."

Every press and media representative was trying to get to him but he only smiled and waved. Tonight was about the stars of the movie not him and he wanted to make sure it stayed that way. He knew it would be a write up somewhere about how he thought he was too good to stop and give an interview to the press.

They made it in and Sean recognized a lot of his industry friends. "You living here now," one of them asked. "I'm still down in Miami." "So So Def is having a mansion party tonight, you should come through." "Alright cool so I'll get up with you later." They walked into the theater and found their seats located on the first row.

The alarm went off and I set it for ten more minutes. My cell phone vibrated across the sink. I got out wrapped towels around my body and hair and read the text message. 'Thinking of only you'. It was from Gene and there was nothing here to stop me from talking to him. I put on the guest robe cut the lights out got into bed and called him.

"Hi good looking," I said. "Ha gorgeous. I didn't want to take the chance of calling again." "It's cool, he went out." "How was your day?" "I shopped all day. Oh my God, Gene we found out

I'm having a boy and I felt him move today." "That's wonderful. What did Sean have to say?" "He was touched. He's so excited about having a son that I almost hate to leave him."

"Are you having second thoughts about coming back here?" I was having second thoughts but I wasn't about to let him know. "No second thoughts, I just hate to hurt him by running away with his unborn son." "Can I be honest with you?" "Of course." "I've fallen in love with you." "You've only known me for a couple of months and besides what would your parents say if you brought an already pregnant woman home."

"I'm sure many men have told you that it doesn't take months to fall in love with someone like you. My parents would just have to understand. I'm willing to deal with any consequences that come with loving you." "That's sweet but he's really crazy and I would hate for you to get hurt because of me." "You let me worry about that." "If you say so. How's the weather there?" "It's been raining all week." "Well good I'm not missing anything." "Oh you're not?" "I'm just playing, you know I miss you."

At that moment I could see his dark chocolate skin and long dreads drenching wet. That was a beautiful picture. "I was a little jealous when you told me you were in Miami with him." "What reason would you have to be jealous?" "He has everything I dream of having from you; your mind, heart and body. I would never try and compete with him but one day I plan to make you forget about him mentally and sexually."

Mentally wouldn't be too much of a challenge but sexually would be damn near impossible. "What do you expect from this relationship," I wanted to know. "Honestly?" "Yes; honestly." "I want a wife. What do you want?" "I want a husband eventually." "At least we're on the same page. What are your plans for tomorrow?" "I'm flying to New York to visit family." "Alone?" "Yes."

I hated lying because lies were always revealed at some point or another. I fell asleep talking to Gene and when I woke up it was five in the morning and Sean had not gotten in. I got up to use the restroom and couldn't get back to sleep. I called Sean to find out where he was. There was no answer he had turned his phone off. He walked in at seven while I was packing up our things for our nine fifteen flight. "I know I told you to have fun but I didn't know that meant staying out until the next morning."

"I ran into this producer I've been trying to book for three months and we left the premiere and went straight to his studio. We've been working all night and I'm tired as hell. Can we take a later flight?" "No you can sleep on the plane." I called valet to bring the car around and the bellman to take our luggage downstairs and load the car.

I tipped them each one hundred dollars and drove to the airport. Traffic was crazy on 285; I just knew we were going to miss our flight. I got off of the interstate and took side roads all the way to Hartsfield-Jackson. We returned the rental car and took a shuttle to curbside check in. I had not slept much last night and he had not slept at all and we were both pass exhaustion. He had on his New York baseball cap and Gucci Shades hoping no one would recognize him.

We made it to the gate thirty minutes before the plane's departure. "I'm going to Starbucks, do you want anything?"

"Nothing I'm fine." "What did you eat last night?" "A turkey sandwich." I walked to Starbucks and ordered Banana Nut Muffins and Bagels with strawberry cream cheese and two large passion fruit teas. He was already sleeping when I walked back. I woke him up and made him eat and drink his tea. I threw away our trash as we boarded the plane. He packed our things in the overhead compartment and fell asleep on my shoulder.

The flight attendant came by to offer breakfast and our choice of beverage but I still had bagels and tea left over from Starbucks. I took out my I-Pod, Vogue Magazine to read upon the new fashions for the season, Sister 2 Sister Magazine to read Jamie's 'not afraid to ask anything' interviews and to check out the latest gossip.

I became so involved with the cover story about an artist's significant other who was trying to take everything they owned and never once rode around for months on a tour bus doing shows day after day without the proper rest or food and staying up all night in the recording studio so that they could reap the benefits and you wanted to take it all. It was a place they told people like that to go, hell. There was no way on God's green earth I would allow my husband to take all or even half of my money he had no hand in making to spend it on himself and his new woman or man while I had to work a 9 to 5 just to maintain.

I packed my magazines away as we descended to land. "Wake up baby we're getting ready to land." "Already?" "We've been flying for almost two hours. You fell asleep soon after boarding." "I'm hitting the bed as soon as we get to mommy's house." We landed at *LaGuardia Airport* at 11:05 a.m. collected our things and caught a cab to Long Island. The second year of signing his recording contract his success was so unsuspected by him; I knew all along he was a born superstar and what he had to offer, the world would never be ready for.

He capped over five million because of the writing he did on his album and ghost writing on other projects that he surprised his mother with a 1.5 million dollar home on Mother's Day. I remember her crying so hard that she was unable to form a single word. He called his mom just before we pulled up. "What's up with the most beautiful lady in the world?" "Oh boy you're so crazy. I was just heading out to the market." "What are you up to today?" "I'm in New York; come outside." She dropped the phone and ran outside just as we were stepping out of the cab.

"My babies, I'm so happy to see you two," she said screaming. She grabbed my hand and we walked towards the house leaving Sean behind to get the rest of the bags. "Mommy, remember me your son?" "You know mommy loves you but my daughter and I have tons of stuff to catch up on." We kissed, hugged and cried all at the same time. We walked into the kitchen and sat around the breakfast bar while I filled her in on every detail that had been going in my life minus the part about the drama that had ended Sean's and I engagement. She touched my stomach and looked at me the way my mother would've looked if I were carrying her grandchild.

"I'm proud of you two; you were high school sweethearts and now look at you; you're starting a family. I know it's not easy being with a man in Sean's line of work. It takes a special woman to love a man that's loved by millions of women." I hadn't thought about it that way, we were starting our very own little family. Sean came in picking his mother up and twirling her around. "You look good mommy." "I'm not suppose to?" "You are, I'm just saying." I smiled at how they were carrying on. You could tell how a man was going to treat you by the way he treated his mother.

"Did Angel tell you we're having a boy?" "No, I was waiting for you." "When is he due?" "November 14th." "Have you decided on any names?" "I wanted to name him after my father but since this is his first son I let him choose the name. I'll find out his name the same time everyone else will."

"Where's Nicole? I wanted to tell all of you at the same time." "Only God knows where that child is." "I'll just wait till she gets here." I was hoping he hadn't chosen a name that my son would be teased for throughout his life. "Would you come on already, we can tell her later." "The name I've chosen for our son is Sean Santos Crews." Tears fell from my eyes. He had included my father's first name into our son's name. "Are you happy?" "Yes, thank you."

"I'm going to be a grandma," mommy said dancing around the kitchen. He looked in the refrigerator and cabinets. "Mommy, you don't have any food in here." "That's why I was headed to the market when you called." He handed her a thousand dollars from the rubber band in his pocket. "I have my own money." "We're going to be here for a week and I want to make sure you have enough long after we're gone."
"Let me put my bag down and I'll go with you." Sean and I walked hand and hand to our room. He closed the door behind us and lifted up my dress. "Your mother is waiting for me." "Just give me

five minutes." "I'm not falling for that." "Okay thirty." "No," I said pulling away. I took my Chanel Clutch out of my bag and left with his mother.

Chapter Twelve

We drove to Costco's and she pulled out a cart and so did I. We agreed to meet at the same spot in an hour's time. She would shop for the meats and I would shop for the vegetables and miscellaneous items. I was on my second cart when we met back up. She was amazed at how I managed to fill both carts to capacity.

"You two must have an expensive grocery bill." "Not really, when he's in town we usually eat out." When everything had been rung up the total came up to eight hundred and seventy dollars. She reached into her purse to get the money. I put my hand on her hand stopping her from taking it out.

"I got it."

"Baby I can't let you do this."

"Mommy, I'm not taking no for an answer." I took my debit card out and swiped it. "Will you get someone to help us out with our things?" "Sure, it may be a minute for me to find someone." "No problem." The cashier called a stocker to register three for customer takeout. "I'm going to walk over to the eatery. Can I get you anything?" "No I'm fine."

While mommy waited for someone I walked over to the food area. I was so hungry that I wanted to purchase everything on the board. I settled for a slice of cheese pizza and a frozen yogurt with mixed berries. A boy that didn't look a day over sixteen came around the corner. "Are you the lady that needed assistance," he said staring me up and down.

"Yes," mommy said trying to get him to focus on the reason he had been called. We each pushed a cart out to the Escalade and begin loading it up. "I got this ladies." "This is a lot of stuff young man." "It's no way I would let such beautiful ladies do any of this work." We stood against the truck talking as the gentleman packed everything inside. "All done ladies," he said closing the trunk.

"Thank you and stay out of trouble handsome," I said handing him two hundred dollars for his troubles. "I think you made a mistake, these are two one hundred dollar bills." "There's no mistake, I know exactly what I put in your hands." "That's what's up," he said standing there in a daze.

I knew the money I handed him was probably more than he made in a week. I wondered how anyone could survive on minimum wage and be happy. I saw my aunt work seven days a week and when payday came everything went to bills or the people she owed. She always told me I was blessed because when you were broke life was a bitch. I got back into the truck and mommy tried to hand me the money for the food.

"Sean gave this money for food." "Well I took care of it so I want you to buy yourself something nice with that." "You do so much for me already." "If it wasn't for you it would be no Sean and if it were no Sean there would be no little Sean." "I couldn't have prayed for a better daughter." We stopped by the Jamaican Restaurant to pick up some food until dinner. I opened my clutch to call Sean to see what he wanted.

I had forgotten my cell in my bag; so I ordered him stew chicken with peas and rice and a slice of rum cake with carrot juice. My cell phone kept going off so Sean got up to turn it off. "I don't know why this girl has a cell phone; the battery's either dead or in one of her millions of designer bags." He noticed a few text messages that hadn't been opened. He flipped opened the phone and read the first message.

'I hope you made it to New York safely. I enjoyed our conversation last night. Hurry home; I miss your pretty face and sweet kisses.' At the bottom of the message it read Gene. After everything he had done to make me happy I still wanted to be with someone else. He felt like a complete ass. He called his mother's phone. "Mommy, where's Angel?" "She's right here, is everything alright?" "Everything's fine. Can I speak with her please?" She handed me the phone and walked off in the other direction.

"Ha baby, what's going on?" "You left your cell phone here and your boyfriend has been leaving you text messages all day." 'Oh shit,' I thought to myself. "Who gave you permission to check my messages?" "I don't need permission. You still talking to that nigga after I told you how I felt about it?"

He was screaming so loud I had to hold the phone away from my ear. I noticed everyone staring at me so I stepped outside. "Baby it's nothing like that." "Forget that. How the hell did he know you were flying to New York?" "I told him when I talked to him last night." "That's why you wanted to stay in so you could talk to him." "I can't talk to you unless you calm down and stop yelling at me." "I'm supposed to be calm when you're carrying my son and another nigga is talking about how he misses your sweet kisses. What kind of man messes with a woman that's carrying another man's baby unless it's his? How do I know that's even my child?"

I hung up in his face not believing what he had just said to me. I walked back inside handed mommy the phone and collected the food. "What's wrong baby?" "He's bugging out over nothing." She talked all the way to Long Island but I didn't hear a word she said. I was too busy thinking what he was going to do when we arrived because he had never spoken to me that way. She pulled in the driveway and opened the garage. He came out and pulled me from the truck. "Boy what are you doing?

You need to help me with all these boxes." "I will, I need to talk to Angel for a sec." I looked into her eyes begging for help. "You sure everything's okay sweetie?"

"Yes," I said really not knowing. "I don't understand what you're so upset about. I'm with you every night not him." He led me to the room and locked the door. I was standing up against the wall and he got so close that I didn't know what he was going to do. All I could think about was protecting my baby. For the first time in eight years I was afraid.

"What the hell are you still sleeping with me for when you have someone else?" I chose to be quiet not wanting to make things worse. "Answer me!" "Sean you're scaring me." "I'm so upset with you right now," he said hitting the wall. "You said you would never hit me." "Is that what you think I'm going to do?" "I don't know."

"I may be pissed off at you but I would never hit you, especially with the child you say is mine." "The child I say is yours? You know I've never been with anyone else." "That's what they all say. I want a blood test," he whispered in my ear as he walked out. He knew I only belonged to him and wanted me to hurt like he was. Here was a man that had it all; looks, brains, money, great personality and last but definitely not least a beast in the bedroom and yet with all of that he was insecure about a man sending me text messages.

I slid down to the floor trying to understand what had just happened. "Where's Angel," mommy asked as he walked back out into the garage. "She's inside." She walked pass the room seeing me sitting on the floor. "What happened?" "I'm so tired of his shit," I said crying in her arms. "Ah baby stop crying." She grabbed my hands helped me up and led me to her room. As I walked by I saw him staring at me. I quickly turned the other way.

We sat on her bed and I told her everything including the part about me catching him and my cousin in bed together and how she confessed the four children she had belonged to him. I even told her about me breaking off our engagement and how I only came back to Miami when he found out the kids weren't his and to stop him from doing anything that would land him in jail. "You've been trying to deal with all of this by yourself?"

"I didn't have anyone else to turn to." "I know that's my son but you always have me." "There's something else." "What is it child?" "When I left Miami I met someone else. Its' never been a romantic relationship strictly friends but he sent me a message on my phone tonight. Sean read it and now he's saying the baby's not his and he wants a blood test. Mommy I swear to you, your son is the first and only man that I have ever been with." "I know and he knows it too," she said still holding me in her arms.

She called for him to come inside the room. He came in and saw me crying. Usually when he saw me cry he would immediately run to me and apologize but this time he avoided looking in my direction. By his demeanor I knew he meant every word he said. "Yes mommy, what is it?" "Sit your ass down." His mother was half his size standing five feet to his six one frame. He knew she didn't care how much money he had or who he was, she would still beat him down like he had stolen something.

"Do you want this girl to lose this baby?" "No ma'am I don't." "Well if you don't get your shit together that's exactly what's going to happen. You can go but I'm not even close to being finished with you." "Will you at least listen to my side of the story?" "You don't have a side." He walked out of the room hurt that he had disappointed his mother. "Angel go get your things you can sleep in here with me tonight."

I walked in the room we were staying in and he was sitting on the bed sending messages through his BlackBerry. I started packing up my things and as I bent over to get my nightclothes it felt as if my baby was going to kick right through my stomach. I grabbed my stomach and he ran over to me. "Get your hands off of me. You don't have to worry about my baby anymore. He's not yours; he's mine." "I know that's my son I was just upset." "That excuse isn't flying with me anymore.

You need to learn how to chew your words before you eat them. I'm so done this time; I'm going to have your mother take me to the airport in the morning." "What about the house in Atlanta, we close next week." "I don't want it. Give it to one of your other girls." "I did that for you; for our son." "We don't need anything from you." "What do you want me to say, I'm sorry."

"No because you don't mean it." "I'm sorry anyway." "Do you honestly think all of this blowing up on me isn't pulling me away and pushing me closer to Gene?

I'd rather raise my son by myself than deal with your crazy ass. You're really messed up in the head, you know that right?" "You don't mean that." I left the room and met his sister at the door. "When did you get here," Nicole said hugging me. "Sean came with you?" "He's in the back." "You look good girl, how long will you be here?" "Until tomorrow but, your brother will be here throughout the week."

"They just opened this new club uptown, you have to let me take you out before you leave." "I can't go clubbing, I'm pregnant." "What? When did this happen? Why didn't anyone tell me?" "We just found out." "Do you already know what you're having?" "A boy and he's due in November." "Well get dressed the least I can do is take you to dinner."

I didn't want to hurt her feelings by refusing her invitation so I went to the back to get dressed. "Where are you going," he asked. "Out with your sister." "That's not going to happen. Nicole parties too much." "We're going to dinner." "I just gave my mother a thousand dollars to buy food what do you need to go out for. I'll cook dinner for everyone." "You can't run my life." "It's not about running your life but I brought you here so I'm responsible for what happens to you while you're with me." He called Nicole into the room to tell her I wasn't going and we were staying in so he could fix dinner for all of us.

She loved her big brother and he was the only person she ever listened to so there was no way she was going to tell him no. He asked me to come with him and assist in the kitchen. He stemmed the rice and baby carrots and cut up the potatoes and I stuffed some of the chicken breasts with onions and rosemary and the others with caramelized granny smith apples. I could burn in the kitchen when I wanted to but our lives were so non- stop that I never had the time anymore. I moved around the kitchen still not speaking to him.

He came up from behind and kissed me on my cheek. "Move!" "Come on mommy, forgive me your man's sorry," he said getting on his knees. "Get Up." "Do you want me to scream it to the world, I'm sorry a nigga's sorry," he yelled sending his mother and sister out of the living room. "I told you about aggravating this child." "Mommy relax I didn't do anything," he said holding both hands in the air. "You okay baby?" "Yes I'm fine." "Damn you women sure do stick together." "And don't you ever forget it," she said.

I set the table and he set the food out. I called everyone in to eat and his mother blessed the food. We held hands closed our eyes and bowed our heads.

"Lord, we come to you as humble as we know how, thanking you for all the blessings that you have bestowed upon this family. I thank you for my children and the new addition to our family. We ask that you bless the hands and hearts of the ones that prepared the food and that it be blessed and covered. We pray this prayer in Jesus name. Amen."

We all said "Amen." We fixed our plates and Sean moved his chair next to mine. "This is good baby," he said. "Yeah Angel this is good. You have to teach me how to make this before you leave," Nicole insisted. "What do you two want to do while you're here?" "I'm flying out tomorrow." "You just got here," Nicole said. "I know but I think it's best that I head back home." "I was so looking forward to having you all to myself this week," mommy said. "Me too," he said rubbing my leg under the table. I didn't want to start an argument at the dinner table so I let his comment fly over my head.

"Please stay, if not for anyone else for me. We have lots of mother and daughter things to do. I never told you this but at your mother's funeral I kissed her and told her not to worry that I would take care of you and love you like my own." That brought everyone to tears. "How come you never told me about that?" "I wanted to keep it to myself until I thought you needed to hear it." How was I supposed to get on a plane after a confession like that?

No one said a word for the remainder of dinner. We cleared our dishes and Nicole loaded the dishwasher. "Come out back with me." "Why?" "I just wanna talk." "Just to talk nothing else." "Nothing else I promise." He picked up a bottle of Corona and we went out back to talk. He knelt down in front of me and broke into tears. "Please don't leave me. I'm nothing without you."

"Is that what you tell all your girls?" "There's no one else only you." "Aren't you tired of the same old re run; I step out of your perfect world, you react on your first emotion then blow up on me and scare the shit out of me and when you come back down to reality you come back crying and begging for forgiveness." "I have a sickness for you. Do you know why I make love to you for hours?" "No but I assume you do that with all your women."

"You're the only one I've ever taken my time with. I've never touched a woman so soft or smelled a woman so sweet. I indulged myself in your sweetness and in the fact that I was the only one you had given it up to. It's like I'm lost inside of you and don't want to be found."

"If you know you're the only one why would you say something so hurtful? You can't just tell someone who you've been in a long-term relationship with that you want a blood test without calling her a whore. If I gave you a hard time why would you think the next man would get it so easy." "I should have never said those things to you.

In my prayers tonight I'll ask God to forgive me and I hope you will too." "You're too jealous and it's driving me crazy." "What man wouldn't be jealous if they had you on their arms?" I swear he could talk the panties off of a nun. "I'm getting cold." "Let's go back inside," he said wrapping his arms around me.

"You two okay now," mommy asked. "We're fine," I said smiling back at her. Once we returned to our room I undressed. "Untie your hair." I let my hair fall to the middle of my back. I walked over to him letting my tongue slipped in and out of his ear. His hands kept going in places I wanted him to stay away from so I tied his hands behind his back and gave him a lap dance until he begged to be untied.

I ripped his shirt off watching the buttons and the three hundred dollars I spent go down the drain knowing he would rather buy a new one than to have the buttons repaired.

"I took the edible cream I bought from the mall out of the bag and sprayed it all over him and my areolas. He latched on devouring the vanilla infused body cream. I kissed him up and down his body. "Damn mommy." The way he moaned and bit his lips told me that I was driving him crazy. I put it on him all night long demanding my respect. I untied him and got up to shower. He grabbed me by my hips ready for round two.

"Where are you going? I haven't even started." "You're being punished now indulge yourself in that." "You can punish me any other night but not tonight. Tell me it's mine," he said burying his face between my thighs. Tonight had nothing to do with lovemaking it was strictly about boning.

"Do you want me," he teased me letting it slip in and out. "Yes," I said. "I don't think you really mean it. Do you want me," he said letting it slip in deeper. "Yes I want you," I said giving in.

"Only me?" "Only you." "Say you'll never leave me." "Sean I cant..." Say you'll never leave me," he said hitting my spot. "I'll never leave you." "And I don't want you talking to that bitch ass nigga no more. Do you understand?" "Yes whatever you say,"

I said kissing him all over his face and sucking on his neck. He stood me up against the wall hitting it from behind and gripping both breasts into his strong hands. "Is this what you wanted?" "I always want you." He turned me around picking me up and taking me on the floor and in the shower. We were so worn out all we could do was lay there and stare up into the ceiling.

"Angel, you sleep?" "Almost." "I'm scared." "Of what," I said yawning. "About being a good farther." "You'll be fine." "I don't know the first thing about kids." "Didn't you interact with Tasha's kids?" "Not really, I saw them and bought them things but I never changed diapers or got up in the middle of the night to fix bottles." "I don't think there's anything that can prepare you for parenthood it's just a natural instinct."

"I just want to be someone he can look up to. When he gets here I plan to take a few years off and let Tommy run everything." "You serious? You would do that for us?" "I would give up my entire career for you guys. Money means nothing without your family there to spend it with you."

"I don't ever want you to worry about the, *what ifs*, because any child would be proud to call you daddy. Let's talk in the morning I'm falling asleep on you." "Good night baby I love you," he said pulling me closer to him. "I love you." We fell asleep snuggled tightly under the covers.